Writing the Critical Essay

AIDS

An **OPPOSING**  **VIEWPOINTS®** **Guide**

Lauri S. Friedman, *Book Editor*

**OPPOSING
VIEWPOINTS®
SERIES**

GREENHAVEN PRESS
A part of Gale, Cengage Learning

GALE
CENGAGE Learning™

Detroit • New York • San Francisco • New Haven, Conn • Waterville, Maine • London

Christine Nasso, *Publisher*
Elizabeth Des Chenes, *Managing Editor*

LIBRARY OF CONGRESS CATALOGING-IN-PUBLICATION DATA

AIDS / Lauri S. Friedman, book editor.
   p. cm. -- (Writing the critical essay: an opposing viewpoints guide)
  Includes bibliographical references and index.
  ISBN 978-0-7377-4802-4 (hardcover)
  1. AIDS (Disease) 2. Essay. I. Friedman, Lauri S.
  RA643.8.A372 2010
  362.196'9792--dc22

2010001286

CONTENTS

Examining the state of writing and how it is taught in the United States was the official purpose of the National Commission on Writing in America's Schools and Colleges. The commission, made up of teachers, school administrators, business leaders, and college and university presidents, released its first report in 2003. "Despite the best efforts of many educators," commissioners argued, "writing has not received the full attention it deserves." Among the findings of the commission was that most fourth-grade students spent less than three hours a week writing, that three-quarters of high school seniors never receive a writing assignment in their history or social studies classes, and that more than 50 percent of first-year students in college have problems writing error-free papers. The commission called for a "cultural sea change" that would increase the emphasis on writing for both elementary and secondary schools. These conclusions have made some educators realize that writing must be emphasized in the curriculum. As colleges are demanding an ever-higher level of writing proficiency from incoming students, schools must respond by making students more competent writers. In response to these concerns, the SAT, an influential standardized test used for college admissions, required an essay for the first time in 2005.

Books in the Writing the Critical Essay: An Opposing Viewpoints Guide series use the patented Opposing Viewpoints format to help students learn to organize ideas and arguments and to write essays using common critical writing techniques. Each book in the series focuses on a particular type of essay writing—including expository, persuasive, descriptive, and narrative—that students learn while being taught both the five-paragraph essay as well as longer pieces of writing that have an opinionated focus. These guides include everything necessary to help students research, outline, draft, edit, and ultimately write successful essays across the curriculum, including essays for the SAT.

Using Opposing Viewpoints

This series is inspired by and builds upon Greenhaven Press's acclaimed Opposing Viewpoints series. As in the parent series, each book in the Writing the Critical Essay series focuses on a timely and controversial social issue that provides lots of opportunities for creating thought-provoking essays. The first section of each volume begins with a brief introductory essay that provides context for the opposing viewpoints that follow. These articles are chosen for their accessibility and clearly stated views. The thesis of each article is made explicit in the article's title and is accentuated by its pairing with an opposing or alternative view. These essays are both models of persuasive writing techniques and valuable research material that students can mine to write their own informed essays. Guided reading and discussion questions help lead students to key ideas and writing techniques presented in the selections.

The second section of each book begins with a preface discussing the format of the essays and examining characteristics of the featured essay type. Model five-paragraph and longer essays then demonstrate that essay type. The essays are annotated so that key writing elements and techniques are pointed out to the student. Sequential, step-by-step exercises help students construct and refine thesis statements; organize material into outlines; analyze and try out writing techniques; write transitions, introductions, and conclusions; and incorporate quotations and other researched material. Ultimately, students construct their own compositions using the designated essay type.

The third section of each volume provides additional research material and writing prompts to help the student. Additional facts about the topic of the book serve as a convenient source of supporting material for essays. Other features help students go beyond the book for their research. Like other Greenhaven Press books, each book in the Writing the Critical Essay series includes bibliographic listings of relevant periodical articles, books, Web sites, and organizations to contact.

Writing the Critical Essay: An Opposing Viewpoints Guide will help students master essay techniques that can be used in any discipline.

HIV/AIDS in America: The Forgotten Epidemic

In the twenty-first century, acquired immune deficiency syndrome (AIDS) and the human immunodeficiency virus (HIV)—the virus that causes AIDS—might be described as the worst health crisis Americans have forgotten about. Despite the fact that the disease continues to claim thousands of lives each year and there are approximately 144 new American infections each day, HIV/AIDS is not an issue that ranks high on Americans' list of priorities. In recent years AIDS in Africa has received a lot more attention, in part because the disease is wreaking the most serious havoc on that continent, more than anywhere else in the world. But, even though many Americans have ceased worrying about it, AIDS continues to be a serious problem in America.

In one sense it is perhaps no surprise that Americans have put HIV/AIDS on the back burner—in recent years they have had to contend with new threats and enemies. For example, America's nearly decade-old war on terrorism has captured the national attention and made terrorists public enemy number one. Likewise, the ongoing wars in Afghanistan and Iraq have occupied policy makers' attention, agendas, and budgets. Compounding the problem is the economic recession that began in 2008, during which public funding for many social welfare programs—such as AIDS prevention and treatment—was drastically cut. Meanwhile, attention to the disease has been upstaged by new health threats posed by the H1N1 "swine flu" virus, cancer, and even global warming. Anthony Fauci, director of the National Institute of Allergy and Infectious Diseases at the National Institutes of Health, thinks America has "a bit of what we call AIDS fatigue, in that you hear about it a lot and it becomes something that doesn't attract or catch your attention the way it used to."[1]

7

Fauci and others also think that to some extent, America's success fighting AIDS has contributed to complacency on the issue. For example, although AIDS researchers have yet to develop a cure for the disease, new drugs have radically changed the lives of HIV-infected people. In the 1980s and 1990s an HIV diagnosis was a veritable death sentence—but now people with HIV are living for decades as a result of advancements in therapy and medication. Consequently, fewer Americans are routinely treated for HIV-related complications, and hospitals and hospices now see fewer AIDS-related patients in their care. As a result, Americans may have come to view AIDS as a "solved" problem, or one that is at least on its way out.

Yet HIV/AIDS is far from being a solved problem. To date, more than a million Americans are carriers of the disease, and more than half a million have died from it. Americans also continue to be infected at an alarming rate—according to the Centers for Disease Control and Prevention (CDC), in 2009 an American was infected with HIV every nine and a half minutes, and about fifty-six thousand new infections occur in the United States each year. Says Fauci, the American public has been lulled "into a complacent state, which is very dangerous." He adds that while the AIDS epidemic has seen certain victories and successes, it is not a conquered disease "to the point that it is now just a trivial problem. It is not a trivial problem by any means."[2]

A 2009 Kaiser Family Foundation poll captured the stunning complacency Americans have developed on the HIV/AIDS issue. The poll found that in 2009 just 45 percent of Americans said they had heard, seen, or read "a lot" or "some" about the problem of HIV/AIDS. In 2004, comparatively, a whopping 70 percent said they had been exposed to "a lot" or "some" stories or information about HIV/AIDS. Other changes included the fact that in 2009 just 6 percent of Americans identified HIV/AIDS as the most urgent health problem facing the

United States—this is compared with 2006, when 17 percent considered HIV/AIDS to be the most urgent health problem facing the United States, and 1995, when 44 percent thought this.

Even more telling are the percentages of Americans who currently view HIV/AIDS as an insignificant problem, even as it continues to ravage their communities. For example, according to the CDC, HIV rates are seven times higher in African Americans than in whites. Yet the percentage of African Americans who consider HIV/AIDS to be an urgent problem has declined since 2006, from 49 percent to 40 percent. The same is true for Latinos, who are three times more likely than whites to contract HIV/AIDS. In 2006, 46 percent of Latinos identified HIV/AIDS as an urgent health problem, while in 2009 only 35 percent did. Even as the disease has ravaged these communities, young people aged eighteen to twenty-nine have expressed decreased concern about it. For example, in 1997, 54 percent of young African Americans were concerned that they might catch the disease; in 2009 only 40 percent were concerned.

Health officials like Ronald O. Valdiserri—the deputy director of the National Center for HIV, STD (sexually transmitted diseases), and TB (tuberculosis) Prevention at the CDC—warn that complacency about HIV/AIDS among high-risk communities and the general population is extremely dangerous. "The threat of AIDS in America is still very real," he says. "Today, HIV transmission is being sustained by factors ranging from excessive optimism about HIV treatments, to inadequate knowledge of HIV status, to increasing use of crystal methamphetamine. The burdens of HIV/AIDS are especially profound for people of color."[3] Since the epidemic rages on, Americans need to be reminded that HIV/AIDS is not a problem that is going away, and certainly not one that has been solved. *Writing the Critical Essay: AIDS* explores this and other controversies related to the disease. Thought-provoking writing exercises and step-by-step instructions help readers write their own five-paragraph cause-and-effect essays on this ongoing and important topic.

Notes

1. Interview with Anthony Fauci, "Despite 'AIDS fatigue,' Americans should care," CNN.com, November 30, 2007. http://edition.cnn.com/2007/HEALTH/conditions/11/30/aids.day.fauci/index.html.

2. Interview with Fauci, "Despite 'AIDS fatigue,' Americans Should Care."

3. Ronald O. Valdiserri, "AIDS at 25: Perspectives and Retrospectives," *Windy City Times*, June 21, 2006. www.windycitymediagroup.com/gay/lesbian/news/ARTICLE.php?AID = 11776.

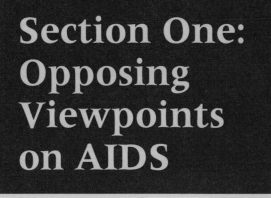

Section One:
Opposing
Viewpoints
on AIDS

Condoms Prevent the Spread of AIDS

George Curry

In the following essay George Curry argues that condoms are vital to the fight against AIDS. He criticizes the pope, who in March 2009 issued a statement saying that condoms are making the AIDS crisis in Africa worse. Curry says the pope's comments are irresponsible—rather than worsening the AIDS epidemic, condoms are one of the only true tools authorities have for fighting the spread of the disease. It is unrealistic to tell people to abstain from sex, says Curry. When they do have sex, they need to know that condoms, when used properly, are 99 percent effective at preventing the transmission of sexually transmitted diseases, including HIV/AIDS. He says people must get comfortable talking about condoms and recommending their use if the battle against AIDS is ever going to be won.

Curry is a columnist for the *Philadelphia Inquirer*, the newspaper where this essay was originally printed.

Consider the following questions:

1. How many Americans does Curry say have died of AIDS since it was first identified in 1981?
2. How many thirteen- to twenty-four-year-olds does the author say are currently living with HIV? How could they have avoided becoming infected, according to Curry?
3. Who issued a statement in 1989 saying that prophylactics (condoms) could effectively fight AIDS?

George Curry, "Condoms Vital to AIDS Fight," *Philadelphia Inquirer*, March 21, 2009. Reproduced by permission.

Pope Benedict XVI touched off a firestorm this week [March 2009] when, in the midst of a discussion about AIDS in Africa, he told reporters, "You can't resolve it with the distribution of condoms. On the contrary, it increases the problem."

We Must Be Willing to Talk About Condoms

While many, including me, disagree with Pope Benedict's assertion that condoms make the problem worse, his willingness to even mention the C-word should be applauded.

At a time when we see commercials on mainstream television for everything from bras to sanitary napkins, many of us still cringe at the mention of condoms, as if they are going to go away if we don't talk about them. Our unease about sex education for young people—and our failure to openly and honestly discuss condom use—is killing us.

According to the Centers for Disease Control and Prevention [CDC] 580,000 Americans have died of AIDS since it was first identified in the United States in 1981. An additional 1.1 million have been infected and are living with HIV, the virus that causes AIDS. The epidemic has disproportionately ravaged blacks, men who have sex with men, and young people.

Adults under the age of 30 and teenagers together accounted for 34 percent of new HIV infections in 2006. Yet, for years, our government has pursued so-called abstinence-only programs. Sure, we should encourage teens to refrain from sexual intercourse until they are married. But despite our strongest urgings, teens are not resisting the urge to have sex.

Young People Must Be Encouraged to Use Protection

A CDC survey of high school students in 2007 found that nearly half admitted having had sexual intercourse. In other research, the CDC estimated that 9.1 million

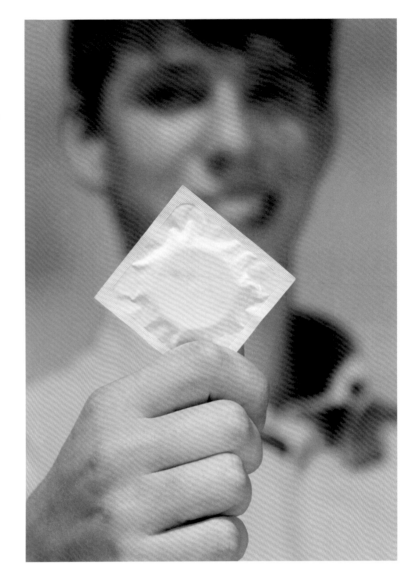

adolescents and young adults were infected with a sexually transmitted disease [STD] for the first time in 2000. Among other things, STDs can cause infertility and cervical cancer in women.

Many parents cannot imagine their teenage sons and daughters being sexually active. But we don't have to imagine it anymore; we know. And now that we know, we must move swiftly to protect young people by encouraging them to use protection when they have sex.

Condoms: A Useful Medical Device

Of course, the ultimate sexually transmitted disease is HIV. About 46,000 people ages 13 to 24 are living with HIV. And chances are that if they had used a condom, they could have avoided infection.

Condoms are classified as medical devices and, as such, are regulated by the Food and Drug Administration [FDA]. The FDA has reported: "The surest way to avoid (STDs) is to not have sex altogether (abstinence). Another way is to limit sex to one partner who also limits his or her sex in the same way (monogamy). Condoms are not 100 percent safe, but, if used properly, will reduce the risk of sexually transmitted diseases, including AIDS. Protecting yourself against the AIDS virus is of special concern because this disease is fatal and has no cure."

That's why the pope's claim that condoms could worsen Africa's AIDS crisis is so dangerous. Not using condoms will spread the disease on a continent that has already seen more than its share of death and misery. Sub-Saharan Africa accounts for 67 percent of all people living with HIV, and it suffered 75 percent of the world's AIDS deaths in 2007.

> ## Condoms Are the Key to Reducing HIV in Africa
>
> Condoms have been shown to not only reduce the rate of HIV transmission but to actually save lives. In Uganda, the ABC principles (abstinence, being faithful and condom use) cut the incidence of and death from HIV/AIDS.
>
> Pius Kamau, "Pope's Words Poison: Comments on AIDS and Condoms Unfortunate," *Denver Post*, March 21, 2009.

AIDS Is Too Dangerous to Dismiss the Importance of Condoms

Although Pope Benedict's comment did nothing to illuminate the problem, there are signs that others in the Roman Catholic community understand the important role condom use plays in addressing the AIDS epidemic.

In 1989, the French bishops were among the first in the church to disagree with the Vatican on AIDS. They issued a statement saying: "The whole population and especially the young should be informed of these risks.

Demonstrators at the Vatican's St. Peter's Square hold up condoms in protest to Pope Benedict XVI's condemning condoms as a means to fight the AIDS epidemic in Africa.

Prophylactic measures exist." In 1996, the French bishops said condom use "can be understood" among the sexually active. Bishops in Germany and other countries have expressed similar positions.

We don't have to look to Africa to see the toll AIDS is taking. Earlier this week, health officials in Washington reported that 3 percent of those examined for HIV tested positive. That's three times the rate considered a "generalized and severe" epidemic. The figures for blacks (4 percent), Latinos (2 percent), and whites (1.4 percent) also constituted "generalized and severe" epidemics.

If we're going to continue to make progress in the fight against AIDS, we need to be more open about the value of using condoms. However uncomfortable it may make us, we must place saving lives ahead of our discomfort.

Analyze the essay:

1. Curry believes that properly using condoms can help prevent the spread of HIV, the virus that causes AIDS. What are some other ways the spread of HIV can be prevented? In your opinion, are these as effective as condom use? Why or why not?

2. Curry believes that lack of condom use has contributed to the AIDS crisis in Africa. How would Edward C. Green, author of the following essay, respond to this claim?

Condoms Are Not Always the Key to Preventing the Spread of AIDS

Edward C. Green

Condoms may not be the best tool in the fight against AIDS, argues Edward C. Green in the following essay. Green says condoms can prevent the spread of AIDS in high-risk or one-time sexual encounters, such as with prostitutes. But in many cases condoms can be misleading—some people think they are 100 percent foolproof, but in reality, condoms break. Thus, condom use may give users a false sense of security, enticing people to engage in riskier types of sex with riskier partners. Furthermore, Green says that condoms are not typically used when people are in long-term relationships. But these are exactly the types of relationships in which AIDS is spreading so rapidly in Africa. African men—even married men—will often have a steady sexual partner outside of their marriage, and it is in these intimate relationships that AIDS is being rapidly transmitted. This is why numerous studies have found condom use to be ineffective at slowing the AIDS epidemic in Africa. Green says that encouraging monogamy will be more effective at reducing AIDS than encouraging condom use.

Green is a senior research scientist at the Harvard School of Public Health.

Consider the following questions:

1. What were the results of a 2003 study by Norman Hearst and Sanny Chen, according to the author?
2. What does the word *intuitively* mean in the context of the essay?
3. How did the African nation of Uganda successfully fight ADS, according to Green?

Edward C. Green, "The Pope May Be Right," *The Washington Post*, March 29, 2009, p. A15. Reproduced by permission of the author.

When Pope Benedict XVI commented this month [March 2009] that condom distribution isn't helping, and may be worsening, the spread of HIV/ADS in Africa, he set off a firestorm of protest. Most non-Catholic commentary has been highly critical of the pope. A cartoon in the *Philadelphia Inquirer*, reprinted in *The [Washington] Post*, showed the pope somewhat ghoulishly praising a throng of sick and dying Africans: "Blessed are the sick, for they have not used condoms."

Yet, in truth, current empirical evidence supports him.

Studies Show Condoms Are Not Working to Reduce AIDS in Africa

We liberals who work in the fields of global HIV/AIDS and family planning take terrible professional risks if we side with the pope on a divisive topic such as this. The condom has become a symbol of freedom and—along

Pope Benedict XVI has publicly stated that condoms are not the answer to Africa's AIDS epidemic, and could make the problem worse.

with contraception—female emancipation, so those who question condom orthodoxy are accused of being against these causes. My comments are only about the question of condoms working to stem the spread of AIDS in Africa's generalized epidemics—nowhere else.

In 2003, Norman Hearst and Sanny Chen of the University of California conducted a condom effectiveness study for the United Nations' AIDS program and found no evidence of condoms working as a primary HIV-prevention measure in Africa. UNAIDS quietly disowned the study. (The authors eventually managed to publish their findings in the quarterly *Studies in Family Planning*.) Since then, major articles in other peer-reviewed journals such as the *Lancet*, *Science* and *BMJ* [the *British Medical Journal*] have confirmed that condoms have not worked as a primary intervention in the population-wide epidemics of Africa. In a 2008 article in *Science* called "Reassessing HIV Prevention" 10 AIDS experts concluded that "consistent condom use has not reached a sufficiently high level, even after many years of widespread and often aggressive promotion, to produce a measurable slowing of new infections in the generalized epidemics of Sub-Saharan Africa."

Let me quickly add that condom promotion *has* worked in countries such as Thailand and Cambodia, where most HIV is transmitted through commercial sex and where it has been possible to enforce a 100 percent condom use policy in brothels (but not outside of them). In theory, condom promotions ought to work everywhere. And intuitively, some condom use ought to

Condoms Cannot Stop AIDS—Only Abstinence Can

Even if used conscientiously (which never happens in public health programmes) the best condoms in the world have a failure rate of around 5 percent. . . . In time, a very large number of the condom-using group will become infected by AIDS. This is not a probability: it is an epidemiological certainty. Even to contemplate having full sexual intercourse, with a rubber sheath a few microns thick as the sole protection against the transmission of one [of] the most deadly diseases the world has ever known, is simply to seek the comforts of a modernistic juju.

Kevin Myers, "Why Pope's Right That Condoms Won't Solve African AIDS Crisis," *Telegraph* (Belfast). March 27, 2009. www.belfasttelegraph .co.uk/opinion/why-popersquos-right-that-condoms-wonrsquot-solve-african-aids-crisis-1424,6666.html.

be better than no use. But that's not what the research in Africa shows.

Why not?

Multiple Relationships Make Condom Use Difficult

One reason is "risk compensation." That is, when people think they're made safe by using condoms at least some of the time, they actually engage in riskier sex.

Another factor is that people seldom use condoms in steady relationships because doing so would imply a lack of trust. (And if condom use rates go up, it's possible we are seeing an increase of casual or commercial sex.) However, it's those ongoing relationships that drive Africa's worst epidemics. In these, most HIV infections are found in general populations, not in high-risk groups such as sex workers, gay men or persons who inject drugs. And in significant proportions of African populations, people have two or more regular sex partners who overlap in time. In Botswana, which has one of the world's highest HIV rates, 43 percent of men and 17 percent of women surveyed had two or more regular sex partners in the previous year.

These ongoing multiple concurrent sex partnerships resemble a giant, invisible web of relationships through which HIV/AIDS spreads. A study in Malawi showed that even though the average number of sexual partners was only slightly over two, fully two-thirds of this population was interconnected through such networks of overlapping, ongoing relationships.

Monogamy Is a Better Strategy

So what has worked in Africa? Strategies that break up these multiple and concurrent sexual networks—or, in plain language, faithful mutual monogamy or at least reduction in numbers of partners, especially concurrent ones. "Closed" or faithful polygamy can work as well.

AIDS Around the World

More than 33 million people are living with AIDS around the world. The highest concentration of HIV-positive people is in southern Africa, where monogamy is not often practiced. Some say that encouraging monogamous relationships can have a bigger impact on reducing AIDS infections than condom use can.

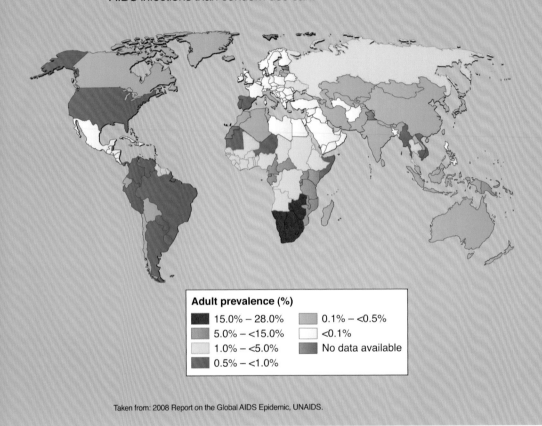

Adult prevalence (%)

■ 15.0% – 28.0%	0.1% – <0.5%
5.0% – <15.0%	□ <0.1%
1.0% – <5.0%	No data available
0.5% – <1.0%	

Taken from: 2008 Report on the Global AIDS Epidemic, UNAIDS.

In Uganda's early, largely home-grown AIDS program, which began in 1986, the focus was on "Sticking to One Partner" or "Zero Grazing" (which meant remaining faithful within a polygamous marriage) and "Loving Faithfully." These simple messages worked. More recently, the two countries with the highest HIV infection rates, Swaziland and Botswana, have both launched campaigns that discourage people from having multiple and concurrent sexual partners.

Don't misunderstand me; I am not anti-condom. All people should have full access to condoms, and condoms should always be a backup strategy for those who will not or cannot remain in a mutually faithful relationship. This was a key point in a 2004 "consensus statement" published and endorsed by some 150 global AIDS experts, including representatives [of] the United Nations, World Health Organization and World Bank. These experts also affirmed that for sexually active adults, the first priority should be to promote mutual fidelity. Moreover, liberals and conservatives agree that condoms cannot address challenges that remain critical in Africa such as cross-generational sex, gender inequality and an end to domestic violence, rape and sexual coercion.

Surely it's time to start providing more evidence-based AIDS prevention in Africa.

Analyze the essay:

1. Green acknowledges that condoms have worked well to reduce the spread of AIDS in countries like Thailand or Cambodia, but says this strategy cannot have the same success in African nations. Why? What is different about Thailand, Cambodia, and African nations?

2. Green is a research scientist at the Harvard School of Public Health. Curry, the author of the previous essay, is a newspaper columnist. Does knowing the background of these two authors influence your opinion of their arguments? Are you more inclined to trust one over the other? Why or why not?

The United States Is Successfully Fighting AIDS Globally

Joseph Loconte

In the following essay Joseph Loconte applauds the United States for successfully fighting the spread of AIDS and for saving the lives of people infected with HIV. He discusses a program called PEPFAR, which was launched by President George W. Bush. This program has spent billions of dollars distributing antiretroviral drugs (drugs that can fight HIV, the virus that causes AIDS) to people in clinics all over the world. Loconte says not only has the spread of AIDS been curbed, but PEPFAR dollars have been used to get lifesaving medicine to HIV-infected people, slowing the progression of their infections or in some cases preventing them from becoming infected at all. Loconte says Americans of all political persuasions should be proud of this monumental humanitarian mission that was sponsored by former President Bush.

Loconte is a senior fellow at Pepperdine University's School of Public Policy and a commentator for National Public Radio.

Consider the following questions:

1. Who is Tatu Msangi, and how does she factor into the author's argument?
2. How many AIDS patients in how many nations does the author say have received lifesaving medicines under the U.S.-sponsored program PEPFAR?
3. What does Loconte say has been crucial to the fight against AIDS in the nation of Uganda? Why?

Joseph Loconte, "Bush's Other War: Fighting AIDS in Africa, and Winning," *The Weekly Standard*, January 30, 2008. Reproduced by permission.

For a few fleeting moments Monday night [January 28, 2008]—what should have been vivid and affecting moments—television coverage of President [George W.] Bush's final State of the Union address fastened on the image of a mother and daughter from Moshi, Tanzania. They sat, their faces alive with hope, in the first lady's [Laura Bush's] box seats. Viewers were not told, and no one seemed inclined to tell them, that Tatu Msangi and her daughter Faith quite literally owe their lives to the Bush administration.

America Is Saving Lives

After Msangi became pregnant, she went to a clinic at the Kilimanjaro Christian Medical Center and learned she was HIV-positive. Five years ago that news typically brought a death sentence in Tanzania, as it does in much of sub-Saharan Africa. But in 2003—over the carping of liberal ideologues and conservative fiscal hawks—Bush launched the most ambitious international health initiative in American history, the $15 billion Emergency Plan

Three-year-old Faith Mang'ehe is the daughter of Tatu Msangi, an HIV-positive nurse. Faith was born HIV-free due to her mother's enrollment in a prevention program sponsored by President Bush's PEPFAR (President's Emergency Plan for AIDS Relief) efforts.

for AIDS Relief (PEPFAR). The Kilimanjaro clinic receives PEPFAR money and anti-retroviral drugs, and Msangi enrolled in their program to prevent HIV transmission between mother and child. In addition to her treatment, her daughter Faith, now two years old, received nevirapine immediately after her birth. Today Faith is free of HIV.

Americans Think the United States Is Successfully Fighting AIDS

A 2009 poll found that Americans believe fighting AIDS was one of the crowning achievements of George W. Bush's presidency, especially compared with other issues.

"Do you believe the United States has made progress, stood still, or lost ground on the following issues during George W. Bush's presidency?"

Issue	Made Progress %	Stood Still %	Lost Ground %	Unsure %
Terrorism	40	20	37	3
Race relations	40	31	25	4
National defense and the military	39	21	36	4
Efforts to fight AIDS	**38**	**31**	**19**	**11**
Education	28	28	42	3
The environment	28	28	42	3
Crime	25	33	39	3
Civil liberties	21	35	38	6
Energy	21	27	49	4
Taxes	16	35	45	4
Immigration	14	28	51	7
Health care	13	33	52	2
The United States's position in the world	12	17	69	3
The economy	5	7	87	1

Taken from: Gallup poll, January 2–4, 2009.

"Protecting our nation from the dangers of a new century requires more than good intelligence and a strong military," Bush said. "It also requires changing the conditions that breed resentment and allow extremists to prey on despair. So America is using its influence to build a freer, more hopeful, and more compassionate world." Under PEPFAR, about 1.4 million AIDS patients in 15 nations in Africa, Asia, and the Caribbean have received life-saving medicines. Bush announced Monday night that he intended to add another $30 billion to the program over the next five years.

Liberals and Conservatives Applaud the Progress

Many on the left, at home and abroad, have reproached the president for his alleged failure to use "soft power" to confront religious extremism and advance U.S. foreign policy goals. Yet here is a supremely humane initiative—inconceivable to foreign policy realists—linked to U.S. security concerns. Bush rightly calls it "a reflection of our national interest and the calling of our conscience." Just think about the number of AIDS orphans that would be scratching for survival without PEPFAR. Millions of rootless young boys cannot be a good thing for any society. Whatever the relationship between poverty and terrorism, this program is probably doing more to check the flow of terrorist recruits than all the diplomatic bloviating [talking] in Brussels, Geneva, and New York put together.

Even the president's most vitriolic critics call his HIV/AIDS policy a remarkable achievement. After Bush signed PEPFAR into law, *New York Times* columnist Nicholas Kristof ripped it as "a war on condoms." But Kristof has since praised the initiative, and a recent *Times* story called it "the most lasting bi-partisan accomplishment of the Bush presidency." Democratic Senator John Kerry labels the program "a tremendous accomplishment for the country." And Paul Zeitz, executive director of the liberal Global AIDS Alliance, believes Bush has ignited a "philosophical revolution" in America's commitment to combating global AIDS and poverty.

Multiple Strategies Are Winning Against AIDS

That's no embellishment. The *Times* article noted, with obvious embarrassment, that before the Bush initiative hardly 50,000 AIDS patients overseas were getting U.S. assistance. The unmentionable fact is that [former president] Bill Clinton—despite a robust economy, budget surpluses, few international crises, and eight interminable years in the White House—never seriously contemplated how America might help the developing world tackle the AIDS pandemic. The plight of AIDS orphans barely appeared on the Clinton radar screen. But if Congress approves the next round of funding, HIV/AIDS treatment will reach 2.5 million people, probably prevent 12 million new infections, and help care for about 5 million orphans and at-risk children. So much for the liberal record on social justice.

PEPFAR's success is partly a result of Bush's decision to mostly bypass bloated and corrupt U.N. bureaucracies and deliver assistance directly to community and faith-based organizations (a concept still resisted by many in the U.S. Agency for International Development). About 80 percent of PEPFAR recipients are indigenous, grass-roots groups: the "armies of compassion" that Bush has extolled since the first days of his administration. In countries such as Uganda, faith-based clinics, supported by local ministers and imams, are crucial in the fight against HIV/AIDS. Unlike many AIDS activist

---

The United States Has Made Important Progress at Home

HIV prevention has already saved countless lives. The annual number of infections dropped dramatically in the 1980s, thanks in large part to the mobilization of the gay community. Recent declines in HIV diagnoses among African Americans and injection drug users offer hope of progress in those hard-hit populations.

Ronald O. Valdiserri. "AIDS at 25: Perspectives and Retrospectives," *Windy City Times*, June 21, 2000. www.windycitymediagroup.com/gay/lesbian/news/ARTICLE.php?AID = 11776.

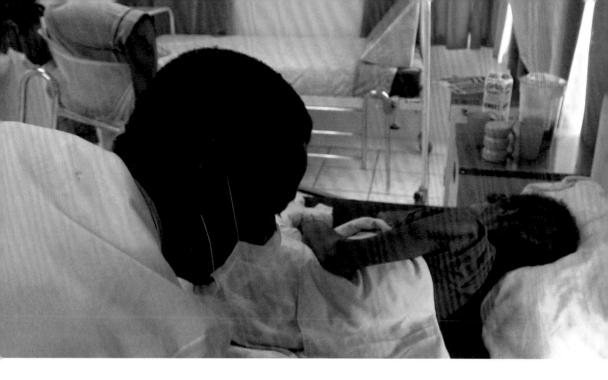

groups or U.N.-sponsored programs, they can effectively challenge risky behaviors that help spread the disease—from prostitution to illicit drug use.

A Most Successful Partnership

By sheer force of will, Bush has orchestrated the most successful partnership of government and international civil society in memory—what is emerging as a medical Marshall Plan for Africa. Presidential hopefuls such as Barack Obama might never admit it, but PEPFAR sure looks like "change we can believe in." Yet, thanks to media indifference and political cynicism, most Americans will never hear the redemptive story of Tatu Msangi, her daughter, or anyone like them, despite their legions. Why disturb the deranged caricature of Bush that shapes the narrative of the liberal establishment?

After all, America's standing in the world, we are told, has sunk to Olympian depths—and it's mostly Bush's fault. Andrew Kohut of the Pew Research Center seems to revel in his predictable findings of the Bush administration's unpopularity in the world, what he calls a "global backlash against the spread of American ideas

The AIDS Care Training and Support Initiative (ACTS) of White River Junction, South Africa, is a recipient of funding from the President's Emergency Plan for AIDS Relief (PEPFAR). The unit provides care, education, and training for staff and community caregivers.

The United States Spends More on AIDS Prevention Each Year

The United States spends billions fighting AIDS at home and abroad.

Federal Funding for HIV/AIDS

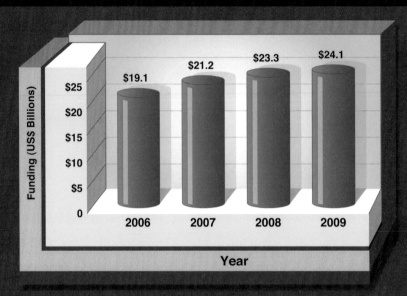

How Is HIV/AIDS Money Spent? (US$ Billions)

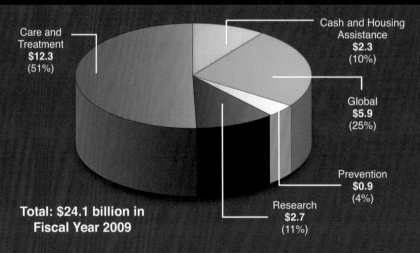

Total: $24.1 billion in Fiscal Year 2009

Taken from: Kaiser Family Foundation, April 2008.

and customs." Yet Kohut mostly ignores the fact that in nine of the ten African nations surveyed in 2007—countries such as Ethiopia, Ghana, Kenya, Nigeria and Uganda—strongly favorable views of the United States are the rule.

The United States Should Be Proud

Dr. Alex Coutinho, a Ugandan AIDS expert, could probably explain why. He told the *Times* that Ugandans are "terrified" that when President Bush leaves office, "the Bush fund" for HIV/ADS will go with him. And he marvels at how little Americans seem to know about the program their government has championed. "Just because it has been done under Bush, it is not something the country should not be proud of."

That might not qualify as an African proverb, but it's an expression of moral clarity that bears repeating during this election season.

Analyze the essay:

1. Loconte quotes from several sources to support the points he makes in his essay. Make a list of everyone he quotes, including their credentials and the nature of their comments. Then analyze how Loconte uses these quotes. Does he use them to support points he makes? Does he use them to mock another person's perspective?

2. To make his argument, Loconte used the story of Tatu Msangi and her daughter, Faith. Reflect on how their stories affected you as you read the essay. Do you think their story helped drive home the point Loconte was trying to make? In what way?

The United States Needs to Do a Lot More to Fight AIDS Globally

Eric Sawyer

In the following essay Eric Sawyer argues that the United States needs to increase its efforts in the global fight against AIDS. Sawyer has been HIV-positive since 1981. He says that although he has successfully been fighting his own progression of the disease, policy makers, government officials, and world leaders have not helped him or many others. The problem, in his opinion, is that the U.S. government and other world leaders are reluctant to make clear funding commitments to programs that have deadlines attached to them. Sawyer thinks the only way the AIDS epidemic can be beaten is if significant amounts of money are contributed to detail-specific programs that have real, reachable milestones. But in his opinion, lawmakers have been reluctant to bind themselves to such plans. Sawyer concludes that millions of people could die unless world leaders step up and commit themselves to specific, action-oriented plans to fight the spread of this terrible disease.

Sawyer is the cofounder of ACT-UP New York, an AIDS activist group. He is also the cofounder of Housing Works, the largest provider of housing for people with AIDS in the United States.

Eric Sawyer, "What 25 Years of AIDS Has Taught Me," CommonDreams.org, June 10, 2006. Reproduced by permission of the author.

Consider the following questions:

1. How many new HIV infections occur each day, according to Sawyer?
2. What did U.S. diplomats do at a 2006 UN General Assembly Special Session on HIV/AIDS that appalled Sawyer?
3. How many people might die of AIDS by 2025, according to the author?

I have been living with symptoms of HIV/AIDS for 25 years, and I am glad to have survived to see this week's [June 2006] marking of the 25th anniversary of the first recognition of the disease. For these many years I have been able to manage my symptoms and contribute to society by educating others about the disease and advocating for stronger public and private action to end the epidemic.

That's why it troubles me so much to see that many of the lessons of the last 25 years of AIDS are being ignored by policymakers and government officials. While my own medical fight against HIV infection is being won, on a global level, the fight is still being lost.

The AIDS Epidemic Is Getting Worse in the United States

The myopic and neglectful policies of President George W. Bush squandered ample opportunities to curb rates of HIV in the U.S. As compared to eight years ago, today's epidemic is larger, growing faster, and more solidly entrenched among low-income men, women, and children.

Mark Ishaug, "High Hopes Await Obama In HIV/AIDS Fight," *Huffington Post*, December 1, 2008. www.huffingtonpost.com/mark-ishaug/high-hopes-await-obama-in_b_147226.html.

People Are Needlessly Dying

Over 11,000 people are infected with HIV for the first time every day, despite clear evidence that, when people understand HIV and have the tools to prevent it, infections can be greatly reduced. Over 8,000 people are dying needless deaths

Some have criticized key players in the former Bush Administration (from left, Condoleeza Rice, Colin Powell, and George W. Bush) for not doing enough to curb the AIDS epidemic.

every day, despite the fact that we now have the medications to keep them alive.

Why is this happening? The central problem is that a key lesson of the past 25 years—the need to keep ourselves honest in this fight by setting clear timetables for reaching basic goals—is being ignored by world leaders.

A False Sense of Progress from World Leaders

Last week's United Nations General Assembly Special Session on HIV/AIDS, which I attended, is a case in point. From the outside, this event seemed to represent more progress in the fight against AIDS. Important statements were made, for instance, about the need to end the violence against women that underlies the epidemic in much of the world. But, the meeting failed to produce the clear road map we need to really confront AIDS, in sharp contrast to the UN plan issued in 2001 on the same issue, which included specific milestones.

As an American, it was especially appalling to witness the role of US diplomats at this meeting. I had to watch as they fought to prevent the UN from including the specific, time-bound goals that African governments and civic groups had called for just one month ago at a summit in Nigeria. One of these was to deliver AIDS treatment to 80% of the people who need it in Africa by 2010. While US Secretary of State Condoleezza Rice has said the US approach to AIDS is "rooted in partnership with Africa," the US insisted this clear target be left out of the UN plan.

AIDS Deaths and Infections Around the World, 2007

Each year millions of people continue to die of and become infected with HIV, the virus that causes AIDS.

Location	Total Infections	New Infections	Deaths
Sub-Saharan Africa	22 million	1.9 million	1.5 million
South and Southeast Asia	4.2 million	330,000	340,000
Latin America	1.7 million	140,000	63,000
Eastern Europe and Central Asia	1.5 million	110,000	58,000
North America	1.2 million	54,000	23,000
East Asia	740,000	52,000	40,000
Western and Central Europe	730,000	27,000	8,000
North Africa and the Middle East	380,000	40,000	27,000
Caribbean	230,000	20,000	14,000
Oceania	74,000	13,000	1,000

Taken from: British Broadcasting Corporation, July 29, 2008.

According to UN projections, AIDS could kill 18 million in China by 2025.

The United States Should Lead the Way in the Global AIDS Fight

Another instance of accountability-avoidance struck me as bordering on nonsensical. The American public does not want to see the US shoulder the whole burden of the fight against AIDS. Since the US is already providing a significant share of the resources needed, it would make sense to include a clear global funding commitment in the UN declaration. Then, that promise could be used to help persuade Japan, Canada, countries in Europe, and others, to increase their contributions.

Yet, oddly, the US government refused to go along with setting such a funding commitment. So, while First Lady Laura Bush told the UN session that "The United States looks forward to working with you, and to finally winning the fight against AIDS," just down the hall US diplomats were insisting the UN statement avoided any commitment to provide the funding needed to actually do this. She also spoke in her address of the benefits of the US contribution to the Global Fund to Fight AIDS, TB and Malaria, while, back in Washington. President Bush has proposed cutting this contribution by 45%.

We Need to Prevent a Nightmare

Platitudes and vague promises will not win the fight against AIDS. AIDS could kill 31 million people in India and 18 million in China by 2025, according to projections by the UN. In Africa, the toll could reach 100 million.

To prevent this nightmare from unfolding, we have to admit that the problem today is not primarily technological or medical. It's that we are still not bringing to this fight the level of seriousness and resolve needed to overcome the problem.

We as people who care about the millions suffering and dying have to go beyond more candlelight memorials for those who have died. Instead, let's declare the next 25 years a zone of zero-tolerance for empty rhetoric and insist on results.

Analyze the essay:

1. Sawyer is HIV-positive. In what way does knowing this about him influence your opinion of his argument? Does it humanize the issue for you? Or does it make you less likely to agree with him because he has so much emotionally invested in the issue? Write two to three sentences on how his HIV status affects your opinion of his argument.

2. Sawyer says the main obstacle in fighting AIDS today is not "technological or medical." What does he mean by this? Do you agree? If so, what pieces of evidence swayed you? If not, why not?

Shopping Campaigns Can Help Fight AIDS

Alex Shoumatoff

Shopping campaigns have accomplished a lot in the global fight against AIDS, argues Alex Shoumatoff in the following essay. He describes a program launched by U2's Bono, called (Red). (Red) works by partnering with popular retailers, such as the Gap, Motorola, and Converse, to sell (Red) products whose proceeds go to benefit AIDS clinics in Africa. Shoumatoff says the money raised through (Red) has helped save and improve thousands of lives in African nations like Rwanda. He says shopping programs are a great way to raise money because consumers get something they want in return for their charity, retailers get to market themselves as charitable and humane, and people suffering from HIV and AIDS get access to the lifesaving medicines they need. Shoumatoff concludes that shopping programs that raise money for medicine and clinics play an important role in the global fight against AIDS.

Shoumatoff is a frequent contributor to *Vanity Fair*, where this essay was originally published. He is also the author of the 1988 book *African Madness*.

Consider the following questions:

1. What celebrities have helped publicize the (Red) campaign?
2. How many health facilities have been sponsored by the Global Fund in Rwanda? How many people have been provided with free anti-HIV medicines?
3. Who is Angélique, and how does she factor in to the author's argument?

Alex Shoumatoff, "The Lazarus Effect," *Vanity Fair*, July 2007. Reproduced by permission of the author.

I am not sure what I expected to find inside the AIDS ward at the Kinyinya Health Center, but it sure wasn't empty beds. This local government facility sits on a hilltop on the outskirts of Rwanda's capital, Kigali, where some 7 percent of the population is infected with H.I.V., the human retrovirus that causes AIDS. So what gives? Where are all the sick people? "All the beds used to be full," says Dr. Fred Mutabazi, who works at the center. "Now there are much fewer patients, because of the ARVs."

First introduced in 1987, anti-retroviral drugs—ARVs for short—block H.I.V.'s assault on the body's immune system. As the drugs have improved, becoming less toxic and easier to take, they have largely turned AIDS in the Western world from a death sentence into a manageable disease. But the drugs' high price—a year's supply can exceed $10,000 in the developed world—has kept them way out of reach for most Africans. In 2003, a coalition of activists led by former president Bill Clinton pulled off the heroic feat of persuading four manufacturers to make ARVs available to developing countries for $140 a year. . . .

While there is still no cure for AIDS, some patients have been restored to vibrant normalcy in just three months.

How Shoppers Have Saved Lives

This medicinal miracle wouldn't be possible without the efforts of foundations such as the Global Fund, which began distributing free ARVs in Rwanda in 2004. The Global Fund gets most of its financing from world governments, but a growing proportion ($25 million by the end of 2006) comes from an altogether unlikely set of benefactors: Western retailers and the shoppers who can't resist them.

I admit to having been skeptical at first about the concept behind (Red). Buy a $170 pair of sunglasses and save the world? Give me a break. Not until I met Bono,

Bono and soccer player Didier Drogba announce the launch of a new partnership between Nike and (Red) on November 30, 2009. The two groups will unite to raise HIV/AIDS awareness through the sale of red-colored products.

the U2 singer, and activist, . . . did I understand what a fiendishly ingenious concept it is. "To change the world we need consumer power; idealists and activists alone will not get the job done," Bono told me. "(Red) is a gateway drug into a bigger movement."

Not A Charity; a Business Model

The idea behind (Red) is simple: participating companies, which so far include American Express, Apple, Armani, Gap, Motorola, and Converse (a subsidiary of Nike), sell (Red)-branded products. Forty percent of the gross profits from those sales go to providing free ARVs to Africans with AIDS. As the Web site Joinred.com puts it in its bluntly worded manifesto:

> (Red) is not a charity. It is simply a business model. You buy (Red) stuff. We get the money, buy the pills and distribute them. They take the pills, stay alive and continue to take care of their families and contribute economically in their communities.
>
> It they don't get the pills, they die. We don't want them to die. We want to give them the pills. And we can. And you can. And it's easy.

For the participating companies themselves, the appeal is strictly business. "What's in it for them is they get new customers, people who will buy your stuff if you do the following thing: give a percentage to the Global Fund," says Bobby Shriver, Bono's partner in (Red).

"It's judo strategy," adds Bono, "using the strength of your opponent to overthrow him." In this case the "opponent" is a criminally imbalanced world economy, where the residents of developed nations live in luxury while those of poor countries are lucky to scrape by. As Bono said at an N.A.A.C.P. event [in 2006], "Where you live should not determine whether you live or die.". . .

An Idea Is Born

One day in early 2004, Bono had a conversation with Robert Rubin, who had been secretary of the Treasury under Clinton, about the difficulty of engaging the American public on development issues. Rubin told him, "You'll never get this issue out there unless you market it like Nike." And with that, the idea was born for a new product line that would exploit the potential of a whole new sector of the U.S. economy.

Bono is the one who named it (Red), a color that brings to mind red alerts, the Red Cross, even the Red Army. The revolutionary undertone was appropriate, for this was a subversive new model in the staid world of cause marketing. By allowing partners to share in the profits, (Red) brought a whole new set of players into the aid game—and gave a scare to some in the nonprofit sector, who worried that "business . . . taking on the patina of philanthropy," as one academic put it, was going to cut into their action.

> ## Using Consumerism to Fight AIDS
>
> Red is the color of emergency. I suppose that's why we chose it. But, Red—Product Red—is a way of making it easy for people in the shopping malls and main streets all over this great country to get AIDS drugs to Africans who can't afford them. . . . This is using the force of consumerism, this tidal wave that's pouring on over our head, and it's just using it to defend the world's most vulnerable. That's it. That simple.
>
> Bono, quoted in Brian Williams, "Bono, Bobby Shriver Hope Americans See Red: Latest Effort to Help AIDS Victims in Africa Leverages Our Buying Power," MSNBC.com, October 13, 2006. www.msnbc.msn.com/id/15253887.

Taking Advertising Dollars and Sending Them to Africa

(Red) targeted the iconic brands: American Express was their first taker. Gap signed on for a (Red) line of clothing, Converse for (Red) sneakers, Motorola for (Red) cell phones, Apple for (Red) iPod Nanos, Armani for (Red) apparel, sunglasses, and wristwatches. "All of our relationships with these companies are with their marketing departments, not their public-relations, social-responsibility, or philanthropy divisions," says Shriver. "Good business is more sustainable than philanthropy, because next year there could be a tsunami and the support you were counting on could go there."

The companies agreed to divert tens of millions of dollar from their marketing budgets into a campaign publicizing (Red) and the African AIDS crisis. Christy Turlington, Steven Spielberg, and Chris Rock were photographed by Annie Leibovitz wearing (Red) clothes from the Gap, Gisele Bündchen posed with a Masai warrior and her (Red) AmEx card, and Kanye West and Penélope Cruz joined Bono on *Oprah* to unveil the line in time for Christmas 2006.

When Charity and Shopping Join Causes

Several well-known retailers sell products as part of the (Red) campaign, which claims to have helped millions of HIV-positive Africans.

American Express

Windows

Apple

Starbucks

Armani

Since 2006:
$130 million raised
2 million people
helped

Hallmark

Bugaboo strollers

Gap

Converse

Dell

Taken from: JoinRed.com, 2009.

Some have criticized (Red) for spending more on marketing than the $25 million it has so far generated for the Global Fund. But, according to Shriver, this accusation is unfounded. In fact, he says, (Red) doesn't spend *any* money on advertising; the splashy campaigns are paid for with money diverted from its partners' existing marketing budgets. He also points out that $25 million is more than China, Australia, and Switzerland combined gave to the Global Fund [in 2006]. . . .

Making a Difference in Rwanda

Of the 136 countries that receive aid from the Global Fund, Rwanda is one of the star performers. In 2004, it became one of the first countries to distribute ARVs with the Global Fund's help, and it launched another country-wide education campaign, urging people to come in and be tested. The Global Fund, which allocates the money raised by (Red), recommended Rwanda as the recipient of the campaign's first grant.

As in many African countries, there had been a terrible stigma attached to being H.I.V.-positive—especially for unmarried girls, since pre-marital sex is taboo for women. But by 2004 just about everyone in Rwanda had seen a family member succumb to AIDS. This destigmatized the disease, and the response to the new campaign was overwhelming. Since the program began, the 122 health facilities sponsored by the Global Fund have tested 635,300 people and provided 14,571 of them with free ARVs. (An additional 20,000 Rwandans receive the drugs from other foundations, including the Bill & Melinda Gates Foundation and PEPFAR [the U.S. President's Emergency Plan for AIDS Relief.) The Global Fund soon launched a similar program in Zambia. . . .

[One] patient, Angélique, 16, started on ARVs four years ago. "She used to be sickly, and now she can go on with her life," Asiimwe says. "She's a good student, fourth in a class of 40, and wants to be a doctor. Both her parents died—she doesn't know how—but she and her

older sister were both probably infected perinatally by their mother when she was carrying them. Her neighbor, an old lady, became her guardian, but even the guardian died of AIDS. Her sister, who is also on ARVs, was taking care of her, but she now is in the hospital herself. We see many children with problems like this." I ask Angélique if she has anything to say to the Westerners who will be reading about her. Her message is "Thank you so much for these ARVs, because otherwise I'd be dead.". . .

Bono speaks with farmers in Mayange, Rwanda, during an African tour to support the Global Fund to fight AIDS.

Shoppers Have Saved Lives and Made a Difference

Thanks to . . . foundations such as the Global Fund, ARVs have been distributed to a remarkable 67 percent of Rwandans who need them. Since 2004, the fund has disbursed $49 million in the country; of that amount, $14.3

million has come from (Red) since its launch last year. But, unlike government aid budgets, the private sector has the advantage of being a largely untapped resource. There is plenty of room for (Red) and programs like it to grow, and plenty of incentive to make them work. . . .

Naturally, the campaign still has its share of skeptics. I spoke to one woman from Montreal who works at Mother Teresa's orphanage in Kigali and is trying to set up housing for child-headed families orphaned by AIDS. "Isn't it pathetic," she reflected, "that to get money out of the rich you have to get them to buy something?" But then there's the view expressed by a Rwandan-exile friend of mine, who recently moved back to Kigali: "Whatever works."

Analyze the essay:

1. Shoumatoff focuses on (Red) products, which are sold in stores in most malls across the country. Have you or someone you know ever seen or bought a (Red) product? Why or why not? Depending on your answer, state whether you think (Red) products are a good way to fight AIDS.

2. Mya Frazier, author of the following essay, says that shopping campaigns like (Red) spend more money on advertising than they are able to bring in to help people with AIDS. How would Shoumatoff respond to this criticism?

Shopping Campaigns Do Not Significantly Fight AIDS

Mya Frazier

In the following essay Mya Frazier reports that shopping campaigns like Bono's (Red) campaign have not raised significant amounts of money to fight AIDS. Frazier says that (Red) has spent far more money advertising its products than it has collected to send to AIDS patients in Africa. She suggests that campaigns like (Red) merely offer shoppers an excuse to feel good about themselves without actually doing something truly charitable. She criticizes the program, saying it benefits retailers more than the people the program is supposed to help. Money would be much better spent, concludes Frazier, if Americans simply donated money to anti-AIDS organizations without making the purchase of an overpriced product part of the equation.

Frazier is a journalist who frequently reports on business and marketing issues.

Consider the following questions:

1. How much had (Red) raised to fight AIDS one year into its program, according to Frazier?
2. How much does Frazier say marketers like Gap, Apple, and Motorola have spent on marketing (Red) products?
3. Who is Mark Rosenman, and how does he factor into the author's argument?

It's been a year since the first Red T-shirts hit Gap shelves in London [in 2006], and a parade of celebrity-splashed events has followed: Steven Spielberg smiling down from billboards in San Francisco; Christy Turlington striking a yoga pose in a *New Yorker* ad; Bono cruising Chicago's Michigan Avenue with Oprah Winfrey, eagerly snapping up Red products; Chris Rock appearing in Motorola TV spots ("Use Red, nobody's dead"); and the Red room at the Grammy Awards. So you'd expect the money raised to be, well, big, right? Maybe $50 million, or even $100 million.

Try again: The tally raised worldwide is $18 million.

A Lot of Hype, Not Much Actual Charity

The disproportionate ratio between the marketing outlay and the money raised is drawing concern among nonprofit watchdogs, cause-marketing experts and even executives in the ad business. It threatens to spur a back-

Retail leaders for Converse, American Express, GAP, and Armani team up with Bono to display products from the (Red) product line to help the Global Fund at the World Economic Forum in Davos, Switzerland.

lash, not just against the Red campaign—which ambitiously set out to change the cause-marketing model by allowing partners to profit from charity—but also for the brands involved.

By any measure, the buzz has been extraordinary and the collective marketing outlay by Gap, Apple and Motorola has been enormous, with some estimates as high as $100 million. Gap alone spent $7.8 million of its $58 million outlay on Red during last year's fourth quarter, according to Nielsen Media Research's Nielsen Adviews.

> ## Shopping Campaigns Are Not the Right Way to Fight AIDS
>
> **Do we really want something as important as H.I.V.-AIDS to be funded by holiday shoppers?**
>
> Brook K. Baker, quoted in Ron Nixon, "Bottom Line for (Red)," *New York Times*, February 6, 2008.

A Very Costly Charity

But contributions don't seem to be living up to the hype. Richard Feachem, executive director of the Global Fund to Fight AIDS, Tuberculosis and Malaria, the recipient of money raised by Red, told *The Boston Globe* in December [2006], "We may be over the $100 million mark by the end of Christmas."

Rajesh Anandan, the Global Fund's head of private-sector partnerships, said Mr. Feachem was misquoted, and defended the efforts by Red to increase the Global Fund's private-sector donations, which totaled just $5 million from 2002 to 2005. (The U.S. Congress just approved a $724 million pledge to the Global Fund, on top of $1.9 billion already given and $650 million from the Bill & Melinda Gates Foundation.)

"Red has done as much as we could have hoped for in the short time it has been up and running," he said, adding: "The launch cost of this kind of campaign is going to be hugely frontloaded. It's a very costly exercise."

Shopping Is Not a Solution

Julie Cordua, VP-marketing at Red and a former Motorola marketing exec and director-buzz marketing at Helio, said

A Long Path

Money generated from shopping campaigns such as (Red) must travel through many different hands before it reaches a person who needs help. Part of the initial donation will be spent as it is passed between different countries, banks, groups, and organizations. Each group involved in the funding process needs to take money for their services, to cover administrative costs such as wages and overheads. There may also be other expenses, such as a bank charge for money to be transferred between countries. For this reason, critics say shopping campaigns do not typically contribute significantly to charitable efforts.

Money spent on a Product Red T-shirt at a Gap store

Global Fund to Fight AIDS, TB, and Malaria

South African Government Health Department

Regional nongovernmental organization

Community organization

Home-based care worker

HIV-victim

Taken from: AVERT, "Funding for the HIV and AIDS Epidemic," August 21, 2009.

Oprah Winfrey and Bono attend a shopping spree in Chicago to promote the (Red) product line to raise awareness and funds to fight AIDS.

the outlay by the program's partners must be understood within the context of the campaign's goal: sustainability. "It's not a charity program of them writing a one-time check. It has to make good business sense for the company so the money will continue to flow to the Global Fund over time." She added that since many of Red's partners haven't closed their books yet on 2006, more funds likely will be added to the $18 million.

But is the rise of philanthropic fashionistas decked out in Red T-shirts and iPods really the best way to save a child dying of AIDS in Africa?

The campaign's inherent appeal to conspicuous consumption has spurred a parody by a group of San Francisco designers and artists, who take issue with Bono's rallying cry. "Shopping is not a solution. Buy less.

Shopping Is a Small Part of a Big Fight

Proceeds from the (Red) campaign go to the Global Fund, an international nonprofit organization that fights AIDS and other diseases. The Global Fund has raised millions of dollars and helped millions of people, but only a small portion of its funding comes from (Red).

Global Fund's Total Money

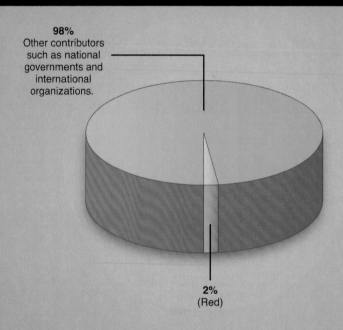

98%
Other contributors such as national governments and international organizations.

2%
(Red)

Taken from: Ron Nixon, "Bottom Line for (Red)," *New York Times*, February 6, 2008.

Give more," is the message at buylesscrap.org, which encourages people to give directly to the Global Fund.

Shopping Is a Distraction

"The Red campaign proposes consumption as the cure to the world's evils," said Ben Davis, creative director at Word Pictures Ideas, co-creator of the site. "Can't we just focus on the real solution—giving money?"

Trent Stamp, president of Charity Navigator, which rates the spending practices of 5,000 nonprofits, said he's concerned about the campaign's impact on the next generation. "The Red campaign can be a good start or it can be a colossal waste of money, and it all depends on whether this edgy, innovative campaign inspires young people to be better citizens or just gives them an excuse to feel good about themselves while they buy an over-priced item they don't really need."

Benefiting Retailers More than Charity

Mark Rosenman, a longtime activist in the nonprofit sector and a public-service professor at the Union Institute & University in Cincinnati, said the disparity between the marketing outlay and the money raised by Red is illustrative of some of the biggest fears of nonprofits in the U.S.

"There is a broadening concern that business is taking on the patina of philanthropy and crowding out philanthropic activity and even substituting for it," he said. "It benefits the for-profit partners much more than the charitable causes."

Analyze the essay:

1. Frazier suggests that a campaign like (Red) is too materialistic to ever meaningfully fight a serious problem like AIDS. Do you agree with her? Why or why not? Cite from the text as part of your answer.

2. Campaigns like (Red) merge the activities of shopping and giving to charity. In your opinion, is this a good model to use when raising money for causes like AIDS research? Should people get something back for their charity? Or should charity's sole reward be the feeling of doing something good for someone else? Explain your opinion on the matter.

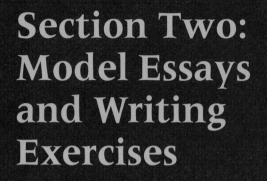

Section Two:
Model Essays
and Writing
Exercises

The Five-Paragraph Essay

An essay is a short piece of writing that discusses or analyzes one topic. The five-paragraph essay is a form commonly used in school assignments and tests. Every five-paragraph essay begins with an *introduction*, ends with a *conclusion*, and features three *supporting paragraphs* in the middle.

The Thesis Statement. The introduction includes the essay's thesis statement. The thesis statement presents the argument or point the author is trying to make about the topic. The essays in this book all have different thesis statements because they are making different arguments about AIDS.

The thesis statement should clearly tell the reader what the essay will be about. A focused thesis statement helps determine what will be in the essay; the subsequent paragraphs are spent developing and supporting its argument.

The Introduction. In addition to presenting the thesis statement, a well-written introductory paragraph captures the attention of the reader and explains why the topic being explored is important. It may provide the reader with background information on the subject matter or feature an anecdote that illustrates a point relevant to the topic. It could also present startling information that clarifies the point of the essay or put forth a contradictory position that the essay will refute. Further techniques for writing an introduction are found later in this section.

The Supporting Paragraphs. The introduction is then followed by three (or more) supporting paragraphs. These are the main body of the essay. Each paragraph presents and develops a *subtopic* that supports the essay's thesis statement. Each subtopic is spearhead-ed by a *topic sentence* and supported by its own facts, details, and examples. The writer can use various kinds of supporting material and details to back up the topic of each supporting paragraph. These may include statistics, quotations from people with special knowledge or exper-tise, historical facts, and anecdotes. A rule of writing is that specific and concrete examples are more convincing than vague, general, or unsupported assertions.

The Conclusion. The conclusion is the paragraph that closes the essay. Its function is to summarize or reiterate the main idea of the essay. It may recall an idea from the introduction or briefly examine the larger implica-tions of the thesis. Because the conclusion is also the last chance a writer has to make an impression on the reader, it is important that it not simply repeat what has been presented elsewhere in the essay but close it in a clear, final, and memorable way.

Although the order of the essay's component para-graphs is important, they do not have to be written in the order presented here. Some writers like to decide on a thesis and write the introduction paragraph first. Other writers like to focus first on the body of the essay and write the introduction and conclusion later.

Pitfalls to Avoid

When writing essays about controversial issues such as AIDS, it is important to remember that disputes over the material are common precisely because there are many different perspectives. Remember to state your argu-ments in careful and measured terms. Evaluate your topic fairly—avoid overstating negative qualities of one perspective or understating positive qualities of another. Use examples, facts, and details to support any asser-tions you make.

The Cause-and-Effect Essay

The previous section of this book provided you with samples of published persuasive writing on AIDS. All were persuasive, or opinion, essays making certain arguments about AIDS. They were also either *cause-and-effect* essays or used cause-and-effect reasoning. This section will focus on writing your own cause-and-effect essay.

Cause and effect is a common method of organizing and explaining ideas and events. Simply put, cause and effect is a relationship between two things in which one thing makes something else happen. The *cause* is the reason why something happens. The *effect* is what happens as a result.

A simple example would be a car not starting because it is out of gas. The lack of gas is the cause; the failure to start is the effect. Another example of cause-and-effect reasoning is found in Viewpoint One. Author George Curry describes why he thinks condoms are necessary to prevent the spread of AIDS in Africa. Failure to use condoms is the cause; the spread of disease is the effect.

Not all cause-and-effect relationships are as clear-cut as these two examples. It can be difficult to determine the cause of an effect, especially when talking about society-wide causes and effects. For example, smoking and cancer have been long associated with each other, but not all cancer patients smoked, and not all smokers get cancer. It took decades of debate and research before the U.S. surgeon general concluded in 1964 that smoking cigarettes causes cancer (and even then, that conclusion was disputed by tobacco companies for many years thereafter). Similarly, in Viewpoint Two, author Edward C. Green argues that a failure to use condoms is *not* the cause of the spread of AIDS in Africa. He argues that a tendency to have multiple long-term relationships has more of an effect on the spread of AIDS on that continent. As this example shows, creating and evaluating cause and effect involves both collecting convincing evidence and exercising critical thinking.

Types of Cause-and-Effect Essays

In general there are three types of cause-and-effect essays. In one type many causes can contribute to a single effect. This effect would be identified in the essay's thesis, and supporting paragraphs would each examine one specific cause. Another type of cause-and-effect essay examines multiple effects from a single cause. The thesis posits that one event or circumstance has multiple results that are explored in the forthcoming paragraphs.

A final type of cause-and-effect essay is one that examines a series of causes and effects—a "chain of events" in which each link is both the effect of what happened before and the cause of what happens next. Model Essay Three in the following section of this book provides one example. The author describes the factors that have caused AIDS to spread so rapidly in Africa. She discusses how the HIV virus originated in Africa and spread to people before it had been identified as a threat. Then it continued to spread because of the cultural habits and beliefs of Africans and also the weakness of their health-care system. These are just a few events in a chain that led to the widespread problem of AIDS in Africa today, and an example of a chain-of-events sequence in which an initial cause can have successive repercussions down the line.

Tips to Remember

In writing argumentative essays about controversial issues such as AIDS, it is important to remember disputes over cause-and-effect relationships are part of the controversy. AIDS and its related issues are complex matters that have multiple effects and multiple causes, and often there is disagreement over what causes what. One needs to be careful and measured in how arguments are expressed. Avoid overstating cause-and-effect relationships if they are unwarranted.

Another pitfall to avoid in writing cause-and-effect essays is to mistake chronology for causation. Just because event X came before event Y does not necessarily mean that X caused Y. In such cases additional evidence may be needed, such as documented studies or similar testimony from many people. Likewise, correlation does not necessarily imply causation. Just because two events happened at the same time does not necessarily mean they are causally related. For example, this issue is at the heart of the debate over whether abstinence-only programs cause or prevent the spread of AIDS. Some argue that because they do not discuss condom use, abstinence-only programs are a *cause* of the spread of the disease; others argue that since abstinence-only programs encourage young people to avoid sex entirely, they *prevent* the spread of the disease. Again, additional evidence is needed to verify the cause-and-effect argument.

In the following section you will read some model essays on AIDS that use cause-and-effect arguments, and you will do exercises that will help you write your own.

Words and Phrases Common in Cause-and-Effect Essays

accordingly	it then follows that
as a result of	since
because	so
consequently	so that
due to	subsequently
for	therefore
for this reason	this is how
if . . . then	thus

The Hope of Antiretrovirals

Editor's Notes The first model essay examines the effects of antiretroviral drugs (ARVs), powerful medications for HIV. The thesis suggests that one event or circumstance—the increased availability of ARVs in poor, AIDS-stricken countries—has had multiple positive effects on people's lives and communities. The text is structured as a five-paragraph essay in which each paragraph outlines a way in which providing antiretroviral drugs has improved people's lives. The author supports her points with relevant facts, anecdotes, and quotes.

The notes in the margin point out key features of the essay and will help you understand how the essay is organized. Also note that all sources are cited using Modern Language Association (MLA) style.* For more information on how to cite your sources, see Appendix C. In addition, consider the following:

1. How does the introduction engage the reader's attention?
2. What cause-and-effect techniques are used in the essay?
3. What purpose do the essay's quotes serve?
4. Does the essay convince you of its point?

Refers to thesis and topic sentences

Refers to supporting details

Paragraph 1

Look at Exercise 3A on introductions. What type of introduction is this? Does it grab your attention?

In Kigali, Rwanda, 7 percent of the population is infected with HIV, the virus that causes AIDS, compared with the United States, where only 0.7 percent of the population is infected. Such a high rate of infection has devastated African communities by breaking down their families, industries, and social structures. When infected mothers or

* Editor's Note: In applying MLA style guidelines in this book, the following simplifications have been made: Parenthetical text citations are confined to direct quotations only; electronic source documentation in the Works Cited list omits date of access, page ranges, and some detailed facts of publication.

fathers die, young children are left orphaned, on their own or in the care of relatives who might be sick themselves. Approximately 160,000 children have been orphaned by AIDS in Rwanda alone. Living with HIV dramatically weakens its victims, making them unable to work or contribute positively to their community. Without healthy people working, communities falter—common goods and services become unavailable, people do not get the health care they need, and the community ends up in a cycle of poverty and death. But an emerging kind medicine—called an antiretroviral drug (ARV)—has, in the areas where it is available, proved very successful in invigorating AIDS-ridden communities and in changing the lives of HIV victims.

This is the essay's thesis statement. It tells the reader what will be explored in the following paragraphs.

Paragraph 2

Antiretroviral drugs work by blocking the virus's attack on the immune system, and they have drastically changed HIV victims' prognoses. One reporter explains that as antiretroviral drugs have become less toxic, easier for sick people to take, and more widely available and affordable, "they have largely turned AIDS in the Western world from a death sentence into a manageable disease." He adds that although antiretroviral drugs do not cure HIV or AIDS, "some patients have been restored to vibrant normalcy in just three months" (Shoumatoff). One such person is an HIV survivor from a village outside of Kigali, who was diagnosed with HIV during routine care for a pregnancy. Three years after receiving antiretroviral drugs, she is strong enough to care for her children and feels like she will survive the disease. "The ARVs have given her new life," says Fred Mutabazi, a doctor at the Kinyinya Health Center in Rwanda where this woman and many others have received the drugs (qtd. in Shoumatoff).

This is the topic sentence of Paragraph 2. Note that all of the paragraph's details fit with or support it.

This quote was taken from Viewpoint Five. When you see striking quotes, save them to support points you make in your essays.

Why do you think the author has included Fred Mutabazi's job title?

Paragraph 3

Antiretrovirals have offered new hope to the people who have been able to gain access to them. One person who has had her life saved by antitretroviral drugs is Angélique, a sixteen-year-old HIV-positive Rwandan who

This is the topic sentence of Paragraph 3 Without reading ahead, take a guess at what the rest of the paragraph will be about.

"However" and "indeed" are transitional words that keep the ideas flowing. See Preface B for a list of transitional words and phrases commonly found in cause-and-effect essays.

was probably infected with the virus as a fetus. Angélique used to be very sick, unable to go to school or work. However, after four years of being on antiretroviral drugs, Angélique not only attends school but is at the top of her class. She has plans to become a doctor. Says Angélique, "Thank you so much for these ARVs, because otherwise I'd be dead" (qtd. in Shoumatoff). Indeed, before ARVs were available, Angélique may not have even lived to see her sixteenth birthday.

Paragraph 4

Specific details such as these help your reader vividly picture your subject. Always write specifically rather than vaguely.

Silvia Ng'andwe is yet another testament to the powerful effect of antiretroviral drugs. In March 2007 this woman from Zambia was photographed looking extremely exhausted, with sallow, haunting eyes. Her shoulders sagged, and she was much too thin for her tall frame. Clearly, the virus was wreaking havoc on her system. But after just forty days on antiretroviral medications, Ng'andwe looked every bit the picture of health—she had gained weight, her skin looked healthy and supple, and her demeanor was vibrant and energetic. Ng'andwe is one of the 1.34 million Africans who are receiving antiretroviral drugs and are learning to live with the disease rather than succumbing to it.

Paragraph 5

Note how the essay's conclusion wraps up the topic in a final, memorable way—without repeating the points made in the essay.

Once people have been strengthened by antiretroviral drugs, they can work to make their communities stronger, more vibrant places. They can also participate in efforts to get their family and community members tested for HIV and help stop the spread of the disease. Though such drugs are expensive for poor people suffering from the disease, it is critical that they be included in international efforts to stem the AIDS epidemic in places like Rwanda and Zambia, where it has struck the hardest.

Works Cited

Shoumatoff, Alex. "The Lazarus Effect." *Vanity Fair* Jul. 2007.

Exercise 1A: Create an Outline from an Existing Essay

It often helps to create an outline of the five-paragraph essay before you write it. The outline can help you organize the information, arguments, and evidence you have gathered during your research.

For this exercise, create an outline that could have been used to write "The Hope of Anti-retrovirals." This "reverse engineering" exercise is meant to familiarize you with how outlines can help classify and arrange information.

To do this you will need to

1. articulate the essay's thesis,
2. pinpoint important pieces of evidence,
3. flag quotes that supported the essay's ideas, and
4. identify key points that supported the argument.

Part of the outline has already been started to give you an idea of the assignment.

Outline

I. Paragraph One
Write the essay's thesis:

II. Paragraph Two
Topic:

    Supporting Detail i.

    Supporting Detail ii. Quote from Fred Mutabazi, a doctor who treats HIV patients.

III. Paragraph Three
Topic:

i. Anecdote of Angélique, a sixteen-year-old HIV-positive Rwandan.

ii.

IV. Paragraph Four
Topic: Silvia Ng'andwe is another testament to the powerful effect of antiretroviral drugs.

i. Description of how ARVs affected Ng'andwe.

ii. Fact about how 1.34 million Africans have received antiretroviral drugs and as a result are learning to live with the disease rather than succumbing to it.

V. Paragraph Five
i. Write the essay's conclusion:

The United States Needs to Spend More on HIV/AIDS Prevention

Editor's Notes The second model essay embodies a more specific form of the cause-and-effect essay: It describes multiple effects from a single action. In this essay, the author argues that providing more money for anti-HIV efforts would have three main effects: to improve HIV-prevention counseling, increase HIV testing, and raise public awareness that this disease continues to constitute an important public health crisis. In clear, distinct paragraphs, the author outlines these different effects and supports her points with facts, statistics, and quotes.

Like you did for the first model essay, take note of the essay's components and how they are organized (the notes in the margins will help you identify the essay's pieces and their purpose).

■ Refers to thesis and topic sentences

□ Refers to supporting details

Paragraph 1

According to the Centers for Disease Control and Prevention (CDC), an American is infected with HIV every nine and a half minutes. This means that about fifty-six thousand new infections occur in the United States each year. Clearly, the HIV/AIDS epidemic is still a huge problem for this country, one that can only be solved by spending more on HIV-prevention efforts. Allocating more money for this effort can have three main effects; improving HIV-prevention counseling, increasing HIV testing, and raising public awareness about this ongoing health crisis.

The essay's introduction should grab the reader's attention and make him or her curious to know more. Did this happen to you while reading this introduction?

This is the essay's thesis statement. It tells the reader what will be argued in the following paragraphs.

Paragraph 2

Additional funding can pay for counseling programs to help people reduce their risk for acquiring HIV. David Holtgrave, a professor in the Department of Health,

This is the topic sentence of Paragraph 2. It is a subset of the essay's thesis. It tells what specific point this paragraph will be about.

Behavior and Society at the Johns Hopkins Bloomberg School of Public Health, thinks counseling programs can be as effective as, or even more effective than, an HIV vaccine. "A renewed investment in HIV prevention does not need to wait for a vaccine or other major new breakthrough," he says. "We have a range of effective HIV prevention tools at our disposal right now that could allow us to make dramatic progress in reducing new infections." Holtgrave believes that among the most important of these tools are counseling programs that help people avoid the behaviors that spread HIV, such as intravenous drug use, unprotected sex, and high-risk sex—especially in high-risk groups such as African Americans and gay and bisexual men. "Only a small percentage of people at risk for HIV are able to access the effective behavior-changing programs that are proven to reduce a person's chances of becoming infected," says Holtgrave—but increased funding can change this.

Paragraph 3

This is the topic sentence of Paragraph 3. Without reading the rest of the paragraph, take a guess at what the paragraph will be about.

This is a *supporting detail*. This information directly supports the topic sentence, helping to prove it true.

More money also needs to be spent on testing centers. According to the CDC, one in five individuals infected with HIV is not aware he or she is carrying the virus. When people do not know they are carriers, they are more likely to continue the behaviors that spread HIV to others. That 20 percent of HIV-infected people are unaware they are carrying the virus means that not enough Americans are getting tested for the disease, either because too few testing centers exist or because people think it is not important to get regularly tested. More funding can solve both of these problems. Additional testing centers can be built to reach people in more places, and testing can be made available to the public for free. Money can also be spent on campaigns that remind all sexually active people—and those who have been exposed to shared or dirty needles—of the importance of getting tested.

Paragraph 4

Finally, money should be spent on campaigns that remind Americans that AIDS continues to be a devastating social problem—a fact that many have apparently forgotten. Indeed, the twenty-first century has brought the challenges of terrorism, war, and recession to America's doorstep, and many have forgotten about HIV/AIDS as they struggle to deal with these new problems. A 2009 Kaiser Family Foundation poll confirmed this reality. For example, the poll found that in 2004, 70 percent of Americans said they had heard, seen, or read "a lot" or "some" about the problem of HIV/AIDS. In 2009, however, just 45 percent said that. Furthermore, just 6 percent of Americans in 2009 identified HIV/AIDS to be the most urgent health problem facing the United States. This is a huge drop from the 17 percent who thought this in 2006 and the 44 percent who thought this in 1995. Since the epidemic rages on, Americans need to be reminded that HIV/AIDS is not a problem that has gone away, and certainly not one that has been solved.

> These poll statistics directly support the paragraph's main idea—that Americans have forgotten that HIV/AIDS is a big problem.

Paragraph 5

According to Holtgrave, "Federal funding for prevention is highly effective. There is a direct correlation between federal dollars spent and national HIV infection rates" (Holtgrave). If the United States can reduce the rate of HIV-infection by putting more money into counseling, testing, and public awareness, it has every obligation to do so. The health and lives of fifty-six thousand Americans are worth every penny.

> Note how the author returns to ideas introduced in Paragraph 1. See Exercise 3A for more on introductions and conclusions.

Works Cited

Holtgrave, David. "To End America's AIDS Crisis, Reinvest in Prevention." *Huffington Post* (11 May 2009), 23 Nov. 2009 < http://www.huffingtonpost.com/david-holt grave/to-end-americas-aids-cris_b_201838.html > .

Exercise 2A: Create an Outline from an Existing Essay

As you did for the first model essay in this section, create an outline that could have been used to write "The United States Needs to Spend More on HIV/AIDS Prevention." Be sure to identify the essay's thesis statement, its supporting ideas, and key pieces of evidence that were used.

Exercise 2B: Create an Outline for Your Own Essay

The second model essay expresses a particular point of view about AIDS. For this exercise, your assignment is to find supporting ideas, choose specific and concrete details, create an outline, and ultimately write a five-paragraph essay making a different, or even opposing, point about AIDS. Your goal is to use cause-and-effect techniques to convince your reader.

Step One: Write a thesis statement.

The following thesis statement would be appropriate for a cause-and-effect essay on how abstinence-only education encourages the spread of AIDS. The essay would focus on the ways in which abstinence-only education causes the spread of AIDS:

> **Abstinence-only education does not adequately prepare people for the sexual realities they will face, leaving them vulnerable to acquiring HIV.**

Or see the sample essay topics suggested in Appendix D for more ideas.

Step Two: Brainstorm pieces of supporting evidence.

Using information from some of the viewpoints in the previous section and from the information found in Section Three of this book, write down three arguments or pieces of evidence that support the thesis statement you selected. Then, for each of these three arguments, write down facts, examples, and details that support it. These could be:

- Statistical information
- Personal memories and anecdotes
- Quotes from experts, peers, or family members
- Observations of people's actions and behaviors
- Specific and concrete details
- Convincing and logical cause-and-effect reasoning

Supporting pieces of evidence for the above sample topic sentence are found in this book, including the following two:

- The fact that HIV can be spread through anal sex. While abstinence-only programs do not encourage anal sex, oftentimes virginity pledgers—students who pledge to stay virgins until marriage—engage in anal sex because they think it "does not count" as sex, or is a way around maintaining their virginity. When they engage in unprotected anal sex (which is likely, since abstinence-only programs do not counsel about condom use), they put themselves at risk for catching HIV.
- Quote from The Body.com, an authoritative HIV/AIDS information resource: "By graduation, 65 percent of all high school seniors report having had sex. Full knowledge of the options available to adolescents, from abstinence to safer sex, is important in empowering young people, influencing the choices they make about sex, and preventing new HIV infections. Abstinence-only programs do not meet the needs of America's youth in their quest for the information and skills necessary to make good decisions and stay healthy."

Step Three: Place the information from Step Two in outline form.

Step Four: Write the arguments or supporting statements in paragraph form.

By now you have three arguments that support the paragraph's thesis statement, as well as supporting material. Use the outline to write out your three supporting arguments in paragraph form. Make sure each paragraph has a topic sentence that states the paragraph's thesis clearly and broadly. Then add supporting sentences that express the facts, quotes, details, and examples that support the paragraph's argument. The paragraph may also have a concluding or summary sentence.

How HIV/AIDS Has Devastated Africa

Editor's Notes The following essay illustrates the third type of cause-and-effect essay: a "chain of events" essay. In this kind of essay, each link in the chain is both the effect of what happened before and the cause of what happens next. In other words, instead of factors A, B, and C causing phenomenon X, the "chain of events" essay describes how A causes B, which then causes C, which in turn results in X. Specifically, the author examines the chain of events that led to AIDS devastating African communities. Chronology—expressing which events come before and which after—plays an important part in this type of essay.

This essay also differs from the previous model essays in that it is longer than five paragraphs. Sometimes five paragraphs are simply not enough to develop an idea adequately. Extending the length of an essay can allow the reader to explore a topic in more depth or to present multiple pieces of evidence that together provide a complete picture of a topic. Longer essays can also help readers discover the complexity of a subject by examining a topic beyond its superficial exterior. Moreover, the ability to write a longer research or position paper is a valuable skill you will need as you advance academically through high school, college, and beyond.

■ Refers to thesis and topic sentences

■ Refers to supporting details

Paragraph 1

In sub-Saharan Africa the HIV/AIDS problem is grave. Despite the fact that Africa is home to just 12 percent of the total world population, the continent accounts for 67 percent of all people living with HIV in the world, and more than 75 percent of the world's deaths from AIDS occur there. According to 2008 data from the international organization UNAIDS, in some countries more than

The essay begins with specific details meant to grab your attention.

71

20 percent of the population is infected. In Botswana, for example, 23.9 percent of the population is infected; in Swaziland, 26.1 percent of the population is infected. A chain reaction of factors has led to the devastatingly high rates of infection in this region of the world.

This is the essay's thesis statement. It tells the reader what will be argued in the following paragraph.

Paragraph 2

The AIDS crisis is so bad in Africa in part because the HIV virus originated there. Scientists believe that HIV originally mutated from a virus called simian immunodeficiency virus (SIV), which has been traced to chimpanzee communities in the nation of Cameroon in the 1930s. According to data collected by a ten-year study concluded in 2005 and published in the journal *Science*, SIV mutated to humans in the form of HIV by the 1940s. By the 1960s about two thousand Africans are believed to have been carrying the virus. All of this means that Africans were the first of the world's humans to be exposed to the virus, and thus have been dealing with exposure for the longest period of time.

The author starts the discussion of AIDS in Africa by going back to the beginning of the problem. This is the first link in the chain.

Paragraph 3

Once HIV mutated, it spread very quickly in Africa due to several cultural factors. For example, in East Africa the virus spread rapidly because of population inequalities between men and women. Many urban areas have far more men than women. Because of this mismatched ratio, people end up having multiple sexual partners, more so than they would if the populations were more evenly balanced. Thus, both men and women experienced high rates of sexual partnerships, which made transfer of the virus easy, rapid, and widespread. Furthermore, the low cultural status of women in some communities made it difficult for them to refuse sexual relations with men. Misconceptions and rumors about the sickness that was spreading—such as that one could become infected simply by looking at a person, or by eating certain foods—only made the situation worse because people did not connect their sexual behavior with transmission of the

What is the topic sentence of Paragraph 3? Look for a sentence that tells generally what the main point of the paragraph is.

disease. Therefore, by the time HIV was solidly identified and better understood, large swaths of Africans had already contracted the disease.

Paragraph 4

The HIV/AIDS epidemic continued to spread further due to the low rate of condom use in sexually active populations. One reason condom use is not as widespread as it could be is because of religious influences in the region. Both Islam and Catholicism are widely practiced in Africa, and neither religion wholeheartedly advocates the use of condoms. "Both Muslim and Christian leaders found prevention campaigns such as condom promotion difficult to reconcile with their teachings, despite prevailing evidence that abstinence and mutual monogamy were perhaps not as common as they would like" (AVERT).

What point in Paragraph 4 does this quote directly support?

Paragraph 5

Indeed, the continued spread of Catholicism in Africa is undeniably connected to the growth of the HIV/AIDS crisis there. As commentator Roland Martin has pointed out, "While Catholicism expands on the continent of Africa, we are seeing the expansion of HIV/AIDS as well." This is mainly because the Catholic Church discourages the use of condoms, for two reasons: because they interfere with the creation of new life and because Catholics believe condoms encourage sexual promiscuity. For these reasons, the Church's official stance is to reject condoms. As a result, condoms are not as widely used in Catholic communities as they are in other sexually active populations, which leads to an increase in HIV infections.

Make a list of all transitional words and phrases that appear in the essay, and note how they keep the ideas in the essay flowing.

Paragraph 6

Where religion has not stigmatized condom use, misconception, myth, and rumor have. For example, in some areas, it is believed that using a condom stifles a man's power. Others believe that condoms are part of a conspiracy to reduce the growth of the population. Sandra

What is the topic sentence of Paragraph 6? How did you recognize it?

Why do you think the author has included Sandra Manuel's job title?

Manuel, a researcher at the University of Cape Town in South Africa, has studied suspicions and myths surrounding condom use in Mozambique. "They thought some of the free condoms were already infected by foreign countries wanting to kill Africans," said Manuel. "The myths are very powerful but they believe them" (qtd. in Swindells). These factors, combined with religious taboos on condom use, have made their widespread adoption challenging.

Paragraph 7

Identify a piece of evidence used to support Paragraph 7's main idea.

Compounding the problem of infrequent condom use is the fact that non-monogamous relationships are very common in some African countries. Indeed, it is very normal for men—even married men—to nave multiple sexual partners. For example, one study found that in Botswana—a country with one of the highest HIV rates in the world—43 percent of men had two or more regular sexual partners the previous year. Similarly, in Malawi—another HIV-ridden African country—a whopping two-thirds of the population was found to be interconnected through overlapping sexual relationships.

Paragraph 8

When people have multiple sexual relationships, the disease spreads faster, transmitting among people who believe they are safe from catching it due to the fact that they are in a serious relationship. For example, many married African women become infected with HIV when their husbands carry on relationships with women outside of the marriage. Reporter Bonnie Erbe paints a portrait of "the typical 'woman' in Africa who contracts the disease. Her profile is that of a teenage virgin sold into marriage against her will and 'betrothed' to a much older man with many lovers who carries AIDS and refuses to use protection."

What point in Paragraph 8 does this quote directly support?

Paragraph 9

The impact that multiple sexual partners has had on the spread of HIV/AIDS in Africa is not found in other regions that have struggled with HIV/AIDS. For example, in nations like Indonesia and Thailand, the disease has been spread more by sex workers and intravenous drug users. But in Africa, "the percentage of female AIDS patients who are prostitutes, or drug addicts, is dwarfed by the percentage who are married women living upstanding lives in their communities" (Erbe). In fact, a 2004 survey by the Guttmacher Institute found that the majority of African women are concerned about contracting HIV from their husband or long-term partner: Almost 60 percent of women said they were concerned about getting HIV from their husbands (compared with just 30 percent of men who said they were concerned about getting HIV from their wives). More women are concerned because men are typically the ones who have relationships outside of marriage.

How is the topic of Paragraph 9 different, but related, to the other topics discussed thus far?

Paragraph 10

A final link in the chain of elements that have worsened the HIV/AIDS epidemic in Africa is the fact that health care in many African communities is difficult to come by and, in some places, of poor quality. Health clinics are often underfunded and understaffed. Many are overcrowded and lack state-of-the-art equipment. Most are located in city centers, dozens of miles from isolated villages, making care difficult to arrange for rural residents. Furthermore, getting tested for HIV is stigmatized in many communities—no one wants others to know that he or she is concerned about having the disease, and people will resist getting tested to protect their image. In addition, in the event people are willing to use condoms or spermicides (which kill sperm and reduce the risk of transmission), these items can be difficult to obtain because they are sold in few places and are given out in clinics, which may be very far away. Finally, drugs that can prevent the acceleration of HIV in the body are outrageously expensive, unaffordable by most people's standards.

What words and phrases have indicated that this is a cause-and-effect essay?

Paragraph 11

Health-care workers and international aid groups are helping to break this chain of events and have met with some success. Education about the importance of using condoms has been somewhat successful, as has distributing antiviral spermicidal foam to married women to use in the event their husband refuses to wear a condom. Writes Erbe, "Foam is the only form of AIDS prevention that young wives completely control and can use without their husbands' permission." Raising money to subsidize the cost of antiretroviral medications—which slow the progression of HIV and can help people live normal, full lives—has also helped to get lifesaving medication into the hands of people suffering from HIV. Even though these drugs will not cure victims of HIV, they can help them feel well enough to take care of their children, help them continue working at their job, and significantly extend their lives, all of which keeps their families and communities from falling into further disarray.

The essay concludes by exploring the ways in which the HIV/AIDS cycle is being broken in Africa. It is a good idea to end your essays by letting your readers know about ongoing efforts to solve a problem.

Works Cited

AVERT "The History of HIV/AIDS in Africa." (12 Nov. 2009) 21 Nov. 2009 < http://www.avert.org/history-aids-africa.htm > .

Erbe, Bonnie. "Pope's Dangerous AIDS Message in Africa: No Condoms." *U.S. News & World Report* 18 Mar. 2009.

Martin, Roland. "Pope Wrong on Condoms." CNN.com (18 Mar. 2009) 21 Nov. 2009 < http://www.cnn.com/2009/POLITICS/03/18/martin.condoms/index.html > .

Swindells, Steve. "Myths Blunt Africa's Fight Against AIDS." Reuters 2 Dec. 2003.

Exercise 3A: Examining Introductions and Conclusions

Every essay features introductory and concluding paragraphs that are used to frame the main ideas being presented. Along with presenting the essay's thesis statement, well-written introductions should grab the attention of the reader and make clear why the topic being explored is important. The conclusion reiterates the essay's thesis and is also the last chance for the writer to make an impression on the reader. Strong introductions and conclusions can greatly enhance an essay's effect on an audience.

The Introduction

There are several techniques that can be used to craft an introductory paragraph. An essay can start with:

- an anecdote: a brief story that illustrates a point relevant to the topic;
- startling information: facts or statistics that elucidate the point of the essay;
- setting up and knocking down a position: a position or claim believed by proponents of one side of a controversy, followed by statements that challenge that claim;
- historical perspective: an example of the way things used to be that leads into a discussion of how or why things work differently now;
- summary information: general introductory information about the topic that feeds into the essay's thesis statement.

Problem One
Reread the introductory paragraphs of the model essays and of the viewpoints in Section One. Identify which of the techniques described above are used in the example essays. How do they grab the attention of the reader? Are their thesis statements clearly presented?

Problem Two
Write an introduction for the essay you have outlined and partially written in Exercise 2B, using one of the techniques described above.

The Conclusion
The conclusion brings the essay to a close by summarizing or returning to its main ideas. Good conclusions, however, go beyond simply repeating these ideas. Strong conclusions explore a topic's broader implications and reiterate why it is important to consider. They may frame the essay by returning to an anecdote featured in the opening paragraph. Or they may close with a quotation or refer back to an event in the essay. In opinionated essays the conclusion can reiterate which side the essay is taking or ask the reader to reconsider a previously held position on the subject.

Problem Three
Reread the concluding paragraphs of the model essays and of the viewpoints in Section One. Which were most effective in driving their arguments home to the reader? What sorts of techniques did they use to do this? Did they appeal emotionally to the reader or bookend an idea or event referenced elsewhere in the essay?

Problem Four
Write a conclusion for the essay you have outlined and partially written in Exercise 2B, using one of the techniques described above.

Exercise 3B: Using Quotations to Enliven Your Essay

No essay is complete without quotations. Get in the habit of using quotes to support at least some of the ideas in your essays. Quotes do not need to appear in every paragraph, but often enough so that the essay contains voices aside from your own. When you write, use quotations to accomplish the following:

- Provide expert advice that you are not necessarily in the position to know about
- Cite lively or passionate passages
- Include a particularly well-written point that gets to the heart of the matter
- Supply statistics or facts that have been derived from someone's research
- Deliver anecdotes that illustrate the point you are trying to make
- Express first-person testimony

Problem One
Reread the essays presented in all sections of this book and find at least one example of each of the above quotation types.

There are a couple of important things to remember when using quotations.

- Note your sources' qualifications and biases. This way your reader can identify the person you have quoted and can put his or her words in context.
- Put any quoted material within proper quotation marks. Failing to attribute quotes to their authors constitutes plagiarism, which is when an author takes someone else's words or ideas and presents them as the author's own. Plagiarism is a very serious infraction and must be avoided at all costs.

Write Your Own Cause-and-Effect Five-Paragraph Essay

Using the information from this book, write your own five-paragraph cause-and-effect essay that deals with AIDS. You can use the resources in this book for information about issues relating to AIDS and how to structure a cause-and-effect essay.

The following steps are suggestions on how to get started.

Step One: Choose your topic.

The first step is to decide what the topic of your cause-and-effect essay will be. Is there any aspect about HIV/AIDS that particularly fascinates you? Is there an issue you strongly support or strongly oppose? Is there a topic to which you feel personally connected? Ask yourself such questions before selecting your essay topic. Refer to Appendix D: Sample Essay Topics if you need help selecting a topic.

Step Two: Write down questions and answers about the topic.

Before you begin writing, you will need to think carefully about what ideas your essay will contain. This is a process known as *brainstorming*. Brainstorming involves asking yourself questions and coming up with ideas to discuss in your essay. Possible questions that will help you with the brainstorming process include:

- Why is this topic important?
- Why should people be interested in this topic?
- How can I make this essay interesting to the reader?
- What question am I going to address in this paragraph or essay?
- What facts, ideas, or quotes can I use to support the answer to my question?

Questions especially for cause-and-effect essays include:

- What are the causes of the topic being examined?
- What are the effects of the topic being examined?

- Are there single or multiple causes?
- Are there single or multiple effects?
- Is a chain reaction or domino series of events involved?

Step Three: Gather facts, ideas, and anecdotes related to your topic.
This book contains several places to find information, including the viewpoints and the appendices. In addition, you may want to research the books, articles, and Web sites listed in Section Three or do additional research in your local library. You can also conduct interviews if you know someone who has a compelling story that would fit well in your essay.

Step Four: Develop a workable thesis statement.
Use what you have written down in steps two and three to help you articulate the main point or argument you want to make in your essay. It should be expressed in a clear sentence and make an arguable or supportable point.

Example:

Focusing on condoms as the sole way of preventing the spread of HIV/AIDS is a grave mistake.

> This could be the thesis statement of a cause-and-effect essay that argues that sex education programs that focus solely on condom use cause the spread of HIV/AIDS and other sexually transmitted diseases. Three distinct paragraphs might argue that HIV is spread when condoms break or are used incorrectly, when married couples cheat on each other, and when intravenous drug users share needles.

Step Five: Write an outline or diagram.
1. Write the thesis statement at the top of the outline.
2. Write roman numerals I, II, and III on the left side of the page, with A, B, and C under each numeral.

3. Next to each roman numeral, write down the best ideas you came up with in Step Three. These should all directly relate to and support the thesis statement.
4. Next to each letter, write down information that supports that particular idea.

Step Six: Write the three supporting paragraphs.
Use your outline to write the three supporting paragraphs. Write down the main idea of each paragraph in sentence form. Do the same thing for the supporting points of information. Each sentence should support the paragraph of the topic. Be sure you have relevant and interesting details, facts, and quotes. Use transitions when you move from idea to idea to keep the text fluid and smooth. Sometimes, although not always, paragraphs can include a concluding or summary sentence that restates the paragraph's argument.

Step Seven: Write the introduction and conclusion.
See Exercise 3A for information on writing introductions and conclusions.

Step Eight: Read and rewrite.
As you read, check your essay for the following:

✔ Does the essay maintain a consistent tone?
✔ Do all paragraphs reinforce your general thesis?
✔ Do all paragraphs flow from one to the other? Do you need to add transition words or phrases?
✔ Have you quoted from reliable, authoritative, and interesting sources?
✔ Is there a sense of progression throughout the essay?
✔ Does the essay get bogged down in too much detail or irrelevant material?
✔ Does your introduction grab the reader's attention?
✔ Does your conclusion reflect on any previously discussed material or give the essay a sense of closure?
✔ Are there any spelling or grammatical errors?

Tips on Writing Effective Cause-and-Effect Essays

- You do not need to include every detail on your subjects. Focus on the most important ones that support your thesis statement.
- Vary your sentence structure; avoid repeating yourself.
- Maintain a professional, objective tone of voice. Avoid sounding uncertain or insulting.
- Anticipate what the reader's counter arguments may be and answer them.
- Use sources that state facts and evidence.
- Avoid assumptions or generalizations without evidence.
- Aim for clear, fluid, well-written sentences that together make up an essay that is informative, interesting, and memorable.

Section Three:
Supporting
Research
Material

Facts About AIDS

Editor's Note: These facts can be used in reports to add credibility when making important arguments.

HIV/AIDS Around the World

According to the 2008 UNAIDS *Report on the Global AIDS Epidemic*:

- Sub-Saharan Africa is the world's region most heavily affected by HIV. In 2008 it accounted for 67 percent of all people living with HIV and for 72 percent of AIDS deaths in 2007.
- As of 2008 there were 30 to 36 million people living with HIV globally.
- The annual number of new HIV infections declined from about 3 million in 2001 to about 2.7 million in 2007.
- In sub-Saharan Africa most national epidemics have stabilized or begun to decline.
- Outside of Africa infections are on the rise in a number of countries.
- Globally, women make up 50 percent of people living with HIV, and men make up the other 50 percent.
- An estimated 370,000 children under the age of fifteen became infected with HIV in 2007.
- Globally, the number of children younger than fifteen living with HIV increased from about 1.6 million in 2001 to 2 million in 2007.
- Almost 90 percent of these children live in sub-Saharan Africa.
- In virtually all regions of the world *except* sub-Saharan Africa, HIV disproportionately affects injecting drug users, men who have sex with men, and sex workers.
- Young people, fifteen to twenty-four years of age account for 45 percent of all new HIV infections.

- While more than 70 percent of young men know that condoms can protect against HIV exposure, only 55 percent of young women cite condom use as an effective prevention strategy.
- Since 2001 the number of people receiving antiretroviral medicines in low- and middle-income countries has increased tenfold.
- By the end of 2007, nearly 3 million people were receiving antiretroviral medicines.
- Without treatment approximately half of all children who became infected with HIV in their mother's womb would die by the age of two.
- HIV is more difficult to diagnose in children than in adults.

Regional Data on Infections and Death, 2007:

- **Sub-Saharan Africa**
  Total infections: 22 million
  New infections: 1.9 million
  Deaths from full-blown AIDS: 1.5 million

- **South and Southeast Asia:**
  Total infections: 4.2 million
  New infections: 330,000
  Deaths from full-blown AIDS: 340,000

- **Latin America:**
  Total infections: 1.7 million
  New infections: 140,000
  Deaths from full-blown AIDS: 63,000

- **Eastern Europe and Central Asia:**
  Total infections: 1.5 million
  New infections: 110,000
  Deaths from full-blown AIDS: 58,000

- **North America:**
  Total infections: 1.2 million
  New infections: 54,000
  Deaths from full-blown AIDS: 23,000

- East Asia:
  Total infections: 740,000
  New infections: 52,000
  Deaths from full-blown AIDS: 40,000

- Western and Central Europe:
  Total infections: 730,000
  New infections: 27,000
  Deaths from full-blown AIDS: 8,000

- North Africa and the Middle East:
  Total infections: 380,000
  New infections: 40,000
  Deaths from full-blown AIDS: 27,000

- Caribbean:
  Total infections: 230,000
  New infections: 20,000
  Deaths from full-blown AIDS: 14,000

- Oceania:
  Total infections: 74,000
  New infections: 13,000
  Deaths from full-blown AIDS: 1,000

HIV/AIDS in the United States

According to the Centers for Disease Control and Prevention (CDC):

- An American contracts HIV every nine and a half minutes.
- There are more than sixty-six thousand new cases of HIV infection each year.
- One in five HIV-positive Americans is unaware he or she is infected with the virus.
- African Americans are seven times more likely than whites to contract HIV.
- Latinos are three times more likely than whites to contract HIV.
- African Americans accounted for 51 percent of the HIV/AIDS diagnoses made in 2007.

- Whites accounted for 29 percent of the HIV/AIDS diagnoses made in 2007.
- Hispanics/Latinos accounted for 18 percent of the HIV/AIDS diagnoses made in 2007.
- Americans aged forty to forty-nine accounted for 27 percent of new HIV cases in 2007.
- Americans aged thirty to thirty-nine accounted for 26 percent of new HIV cases in 2007.
- Americans aged twenty to twenty-nine accounted for 25 percent of new HIV cases in 2007.
- Nearly 75 percent of Americans diagnosed with HIV in 2007 were male.
- Fifty-three percent of all HIV diagnoses were the result of men having sex with men.
- Thirty-two percent were the result of high-risk heterosexual contact.
- Seventeen percent were the result of injection drug use.
- Three percent were the result of male-to-male sexual contact *and* injection drug use.
- One percent was the result of another type of interaction.
- It would take $4.8 billion over five years to reduce the annual number of new HIV infections in the United States.
- Only about 4 percent of HIV/AIDS funding is devoted to prevention programs.

Medical advances and improvements in drugs and treatment have slowed the progression of HIV infection to AIDS. According to the CDC, this has helped prevent diagnoses of and deaths from AIDS:

- In 2007 there were 35,695 AIDS diagnoses, compared with 38,893 in 2003.
- In 2007 there were 14,989 deaths from AIDS, compared with 17,082 in 2003.
- In 2007 there were 455,636 persons living with AIDS, compared with 372,136 in 2003.

American Opinions About HIV/AIDS

According to a 2009 poll by the Kaiser Family Foundation:

- Six percent of Americans think HIV/AIDS is the most urgent health problem facing the nation (compared with 44 percent in 1995).
- Seventeen percent of Americans say HIV/AIDS is an urgent problem (compared with 23 percent in 2006).
- Forty percent of African Americans say HIV/AIDS is an urgent problem (compared with 49 percent in 2006).
- Thirty-five percent of Latinos say HIV/AIDS is an urgent problem (compared with 46 percent in 2006)
- Seventeen percent of eighteen-to-twenty-nine-year-old Americans say they are personally concerned about becoming infected with HIV (compared with 30 percent in 1997).
- Forty percent of eighteen-to-twenty-nine-year-old African Americans say they are personally concerned about becoming infected with HIV (compared with 54 percent in 1997).
- More than half (53 percent) of non-elderly adults say they have been tested at some point in their lives for HIV.
- Nineteen percent have been tested within the last year.
- Thirty percent of young adults say they have been tested within the past year.
- Forty-seven percent of young African Americans say they have been tested within the past year.
- Half of the public thinks that the federal government is spending too little on domestic HIV/AIDS.
- Five percent say the government spends too much on HIV/AIDS.
- More than a third (36 percent) of Americans say they have personally donated money to an HIV/AIDS-related charity.

Myths and perceptions about HIV/AIDS from the 2009 Kaiser Family Foundation poll:

- Forty-four percent of Americans say they would be very comfortable working with someone who has HIV/AIDS (compared with 32 percent in 1997).
- Fifty-one percent of Americans say they would be uncomfortable having their food prepared by someone who is HIV-positive.
- Twenty-seven percent of Americans wrongly believe that HIV can be transmitted by sharing a drinking glass.
- Seventeen percent of Americans wrongly believe that HIV can be transmitted by touching a toilet seat.
- Fourteen percent of Americans wrongly believe that HIV can be transmitted by swimming in a pool with an HIV-positive person.
- Nearly one in five Americans—18 percent—is unaware that there is no cure for AIDS.
- Nearly a quarter of Americans—24 percent—wrongly believe that there is a vaccine available to prevent HIV infection or are unsure if there is one (there is not).
- Thirty-six percent of African Americans wrongly believe there is a vaccine that can prevent HIV infection.
- Thirty percent of African Americans wrongly believe that there are drugs that can cure HIV and AIDS.

According to a 2009 Gallup poll:

- Thirty-eight percent of Americans think the United States made progress fighting AIDS from 2000 to 2008 when George W. Bush was president.
- Thirty-one percent of Americans think the United States stood still on/made no progress on efforts to fight AIDS during this time.
- Nineteen percent of Americans think the United States lost ground fighting AIDS during this time.
- Eleven percent of Americans were unsure.

Finding and Using Sources of Information

No matter what type of essay you are writing, it is necessary to find information to support your point of view. You can use sources such as books, magazine articles, newspaper articles, and online articles.

Using Books and Articles

You can find books and articles in a library by using the library's computer or cataloging system. If you are not sure how to use these resources, ask a librarian to help you. You can also use a computer to find many magazine articles and other articles written specifically for the Internet.

You are likely to find a lot more information than you can possibly use in your essay, so your first task is to narrow it down to what is likely to be most usable. Look at book and article titles. Look at book chapter titles, and examine the book's index to see if it contains information on the specific topic you want to write about. (For example, if you want to write about whether condoms can reduce the spread of AIDS and you find a book about sex education, check the chapter titles and index to be sure it contains information about condoms and AIDS before you bother to check out the book.)

For a five-paragraph essay, you do not need a great deal of supporting information, so quickly try to narrow down your materials to a few good books and magazine or Internet articles. You do not need dozens. You might even find that one or two good books or articles contain all the information you need.

You probably do not have time to read an entire book, so find the chapters or sections that relate to your topic and skim these. When you find useful information, copy it onto a note card or notebook. You should look for supporting facts, statistics, quotations, and examples.

Using the Internet

When you select your supporting information, it is important that you evaluate its source. This is especially important with information you find on the Internet. Because nearly anyone can put information on the Internet, there is as much bad information as good information. Before using Internet information—or any information—try to determine if the source seems to be reliable. Is the author or Internet site sponsored by a legitimate organization? Is it from a government source? Does the author have any special knowledge or training relating to the topic you are looking up? Does the article give any indication of where its information comes from?

Using Your Supporting Information

When you use supporting information from a book, article, interview, or other source, there are three important things to remember:

1. *Make it clear whether you are using a direct quotation or a paraphrase.* If you copy information directly from your source, you are quoting it. You must put quotation marks around the information and tell where the information comes from. If you put the information in your own words, you are paraphrasing it.

   Here is an example of a using a quotation:

   Reporter Ron Nixon describes conditions at a Rwandan health clinic before the arrival of anti-retroviral drugs: "Patients, unable to find care elsewhere, flowed in from every corner of the country. And if one of them was fortunate enough to find a bed here, she often had to share it." But today many of these patients have been successfully treated, and the clinic's waiting room has thus been transformed into a more cheerful, manageable place. Doctors now have more time to see patients who have yet to benefit from these widely successful drugs.

Here is an example of a brief paraphrase of the same passage:

> Before the arrival of antiretroviral drugs, clinics like the Treatment and Research AIDS Center in Kigali, Rwanda, could barely cope with the influx of sick people. The center was overwhelmed with patients seeking treatment, many of whom had to share a bed with another patient. But today many of these patients have been successfully treated, and the clinic's waiting room has thus been transformed into a more cheerful, manageable place. Doctors now have more time to see patients who have yet to benefit from these widely successful drugs.

2. *Use the information fairly*. Be careful to use supporting information in the way the author intended it. For example, it is unfair to quote an author as saying, "Condoms may prevent the spread of HIV," when he or she intended to say, "Condoms may prevent the spread of HIV in a few cases, but abstaining from sex is the only behavior that can halt the spread of the epidemic entirely." This is called taking information out of context. This is using supporting evidence unfairly.

3. *Give credit where credit is due*. Giving credit is known as citing. You must use citations when you use someone else's information, but not every piece of supporting information needs a citation.

   - If the supporting information is general knowledge—that is, it can be found in many sources—you do not have to cite your source.
   - If you directly quote a source, you must cite it.
   - If you paraphrase information from a specific source, you must cite it.

If you do not use citations where you should, you are *plagiarizing*—or stealing—someone else's work.

Citing Your Sources

There are a number of ways to cite your sources. Your teacher will probably want you to do it in one of three ways:

- Informal: As in the example in number 1 above, tell where you got the information as you present it in the text of your essay.
- Informal list: At the end of your essay, place an unnumbered list of all the sources you used. This tells the reader where, in general, your information came from.
- Formal: Use numbered footnotes or endnotes. Footnotes or endnotes are generally placed at the end of an article or essay, although they may be placed elsewhere depending on your teacher's requirements.

Works Cited

Nixon, Ron. "Bottom Line for (Red)." *New York Times* 6 Feb. 2008.

Using MLA Style to Create a Works Cited List

You will probably need to create a list of works cited for your paper. These include materials that you quoted from, relied heavily on, or consulted to write your paper. There are several different ways to structure these references. The following examples are based on Modern Language Association (MLA) style, one of the major citation styles used by writers.

Book Entries

For most book entries you will need the author's name, the book's title, where it was published, what company published it, and the year it was published. This information is usually found on the inside of the book. Variations on book entries include the following:

A book by a single author:
> Axworthy, Michael. *A History of Iran: Empire of the Mind.* New York: Basic Books, 2008.

Two or more books by the same author:
> Pollan, Michael. *In Defense of Food: An Eater's Manifesto.* New York: Penguin, 2009.
> ———. *The Omnivore's Dilemma.* New York: Penguin, 2006.

A book by two or more authors:
> Ronald, Pamela C., and R.W. Adamchak. *Tomorrow's Table: Organic Farming, Genetics, and the Future of Food.* New York: Oxford University Press, 2008.

A book with an editor:
> Friedman, Lauri S., ed. *Introducing Issues with Opposing Viewpoints: War*. Detroit: Greenhaven, 2009.

Periodical and Newspaper Entries

Entries for sources found in periodicals and newspapers are cited a bit differently than books. For one, these sources usually have a title and a publication name. They also may have specific dates and page numbers. Unlike book entries, you do not need to list where newspapers or periodicals are published or what company publishes them.

An article from a periodical:
> Hannum, William H., Gerald E. Marsh, and George S. Stanford. "Smarter Use of Nuclear Waste." *Scientific American* Dec. 2005: 84–91.

An unsigned article from a periodical:
> "The Chinese Disease? The Rapid Spread of Syphilis in China." *Global Agenda* 14 Jan. 2007.

An article from a newspaper:
> Weiss, Rick. "Can Food from Cloned Animals Be Called Organic?" *Washington Post* 29 Jan. 2008: A06.

Internet Sources

To document a source you found online, try to provide as much information on it as possible, including the author's name, the title of the document, date of publication or of last revision, the URL, and your date of access.

A Web source:
> De Seno, Tommy. "*Roe vs. Wade* and the Rights of the Father." Fox Forum.com (22 Jan. 2009) 20 May 2009 < http://foxforum.blogs.foxnews .com/2009/01/22/deseno_roe_wade/ > .

Your teacher will tell you exactly how information should be cited in your essay. Generally, you will at least need the original author's name and the name of the article or other publication.

Be sure you know exactly what information your teacher requires before you start looking for your supporting information so that you know what information to include with your notes.

Sample Essay Topics

AIDS Is a Global Health Crisis

The AIDS Crisis Has Been Exaggerated

AIDS Is a Serious Health Problem in America

The AIDS Epidemic Has Improved in America

The AIDS Crisis in Africa

The AIDS Crisis in Asia

How the AIDS Crisis Differs Around the World

Abstinence-Only Education Can Prevent the Spread of AIDS

Abstinence-Only Education Causes the Spread of AIDS

Condoms Prevent the Spread of AIDS

Condoms Cannot Prevent the Spread of AIDS

Condoms Should Be Given Out for Free to Prevent the Spread of AIDS

Condoms Should Not Be Given Out for Free

Condom Use Should Be Encouraged in All Societies

The Use of Condoms Is Not Likely to Be Adopted in Some Societies

AIDS-Relief Efforts Should Focus on Laxer Morals

AIDS-Relief Efforts Should Focus on Poverty

AIDS-Relief Efforts Should Focus on Prostitution

AIDS-Relief Efforts Should Focus on Drug Abuse

AIDS-Relief Efforts Should Focus on Encouraging Monogamy

AIDS-Relief Efforts Should Focus on At-Risk Populations Such as African Americans and Homosexuals

Africa Needs More Foreign Money to Fight AIDS

Foreign Money to Africa Does Not Help Fight AIDS

Organizations to Contact

The editor has compiled the following list of organizations concerned with the issues debated in this book. The descriptions are derived from materials provided by the organizations. All have publications or information available for interested readers. The list was compiled on the date of publication of the present volume; the information provided here may change. Be aware that many organizations take several weeks or longer to respond to inquiries, so allow as much time as possible.

Adolescent AIDS Program
Children's Hospital at Montefiore Medical Center
111 E. 210th St. Bronx, NY 10467
(718) 882-0232 • e-mail: info@adolescentaids.org
Web site: www.adolescentaids.org

The Adolescent AIDS Program opened in 1987 as the first program to provide medical and psychosocial care to HIV-positive and at-risk adolescents aged thirteen to twenty-one. It also conducts research and provides education for health professionals and students about AIDS and adolescents. The program has many position papers available concerning AIDS and teenagers.

AIDS Coalition to Unleash Power (ACT UP)
332 Bleecker St., Ste. G5 New York, NY 10014
Web site: www.actupny.org

This is a national organization composed of individuals committed to ending AIDS. Its members believe that politicians, doctors, and researchers are not doing enough to combat the disease. To increase public awareness of AIDS, ACT UP members meet with government officials, hold protests, distribute medical information, and publish various materials on the topic. The group's Web site links to the New York group, but ACT UP chapters are active in Philadelphia, San Francisco, and other American cities.

AIDS Vaccine Advocacy Coalition (AVAC)

101 W. Twenty-third St., #2227 New York, NY 10011
(212) 367-1279 • e-mail: avac@avac.org
Web Site: www.avac.org

Founded in 1995, AVAC is an international nonprofit organization that uses education, policy analysis, advocacy, and community mobilization to accelerate the ethical development and eventual global delivery of AIDS vaccines and other new HIV prevention options as part of a comprehensive response to the pandemic. Numerous publications and educational resources are available for download on the group's Web site.

Alive and Well AIDS Alternatives

11684 Ventura Blvd. Studio City, CA 91604
(818) 780-1875 • e-mail: info@aliveandwell.org
Web site: www.aliveandwell.org

This nonprofit support, education, and health advocacy network was founded in 1995 by a group of HIV-positive men and women. Their mission is to inspire productive dialogue and vital research in order to bring about healthy solutions to the global tragedy of AIDS.

American Foundation for AIDS Research (amfAR)

120 Wall St., 13th Fl. New York, NY 10005-3908
(212) 806-1600 • Web site: http://amfar.org

The American Foundation for AIDS Research is dedicated to ending the global AIDS epidemic through innovative research. It plays an important role in accelerating the pace of HIV/AIDS research and achieving real breakthroughs. Since 1985, amfAR has invested nearly $290 million in its mission and has awarded grants to more than two thousand research teams worldwide. It publishes several monographs, compendiums, journals, and periodic publications, many of which are available for download on its Web site.

Centers for Disease Control and Prevention, National Prevention Information Network (NPIN)

PO Box 6003 Rockville, MD 20849-6003
(800) 458-5231 • e-mail: info@cdcnpin.org
Web site: www.cdcnpin.org

The NPIN is the U.S. reference and referral service for information on HIV/AIDS, viral hepatitis, sexually transmitted diseases (STDs), and tuberculosis (TB). The NPIN collects, catalogs, processes, and electronically disseminates materials and information on HIV/AIDS, viral hepatitis, STDs, and TB to organizations and people working in those disease fields in international, national, state, and local settings.

Family Research Council (FRC)

801 G St. NW Washington, DC 20001
(202) 393-2100 • e-mail: corrdept@frc.org
Web site: www.frc.org

The Family Research Council is a research, resource, and education organization that promotes the traditional family. It opposes sex education and condom distribution programs in schools, believing they encourage sexual promiscuity and lead to the spread of AIDS.

Gay Men's Health Crisis

The Tisch Building, 119 W. Twenty-fourth St.
New York, NY 10011 • (212) 367-1000
Web site www.gmhc.org

Founded in 1982, the Gay Men's Health Crisis provides support services, education, and advocacy for men, women, and children with AIDS. Its Web site contains downloadable reports, program information, and statistics, along with information about volunteer and activist events.

Global AIDS Interfaith Alliance (GAIA)
The Presidio of San Francisco PO Box 29110
San Francisco, CA 94129-0110
(415) 461-7196 • e-mail: info@thegaia.org
Web site: www.thegaia.org

This organization delivers HIV-related and basic health services to rural villages and health facilities in Africa. GAIA is currently at work in Malawi, a small country located in sub-Saharan Africa at the epicenter of the global HIV/AIDS epidemic where 80,000 people die of AIDS-related illnesses each year and over 550,000 children have been orphaned.

Harvard AIDS Institute (HAI)
651 Huntington Ave. Boston, MA 02115
(617) 432-4400 • Web site: www.aids.harvard.edu

The HAI is dedicated to promoting research, education, and leadership to end the AIDS epidemic. It partners with organizations in Africa and other regions of the world to develop sustained education and training programs. As the number of AIDS cases continues to escalate disproportionately in Africa and other resource-scarce settings, the HAI has directed its research efforts toward developing prevention and treatment strategies to stem the epidemic in these regions. Information about the HAI's efforts is available on its Web site.

International AIDS Vaccine Initiative (IAVI)
110 William St., Fl. 27 New York, NY 10038-3901
(212) 847-1111 • Web site: www.iavi.org

The IAVI's mission is to support the development of preventive AIDS vaccines that are safe, effective, and accessible. To this end, it invests in the research and clinical assessment of candidate vaccines against strains of HIV that are prevalent in the developing world, where some 95 percent of new HIV infections occur. It puts out many publications about its efforts that are available for download on its Web site.

International Council of AIDS Services Organizations (ICASO)
65 Wellesley St. E., Ste. 403 Toronto, ON
M4Y 1G7 Canada • (416) 921-0018
Web site: www.icaso.org

The ICASO's mission is to mobilize and support diverse community organizations to build an effective global response to HIV and AIDS. The group seeks to help people living with and affected by HIV and AIDS to enjoy life free from stigma, discrimination, and persecution and to have access to prevention, treatment, and care. The ICASO network operates globally, regionally, and locally and reaches over one hundred countries. More information about its activities is available on its Web site, where numerous publications are available for download.

Joint United Nations Programme on HIV/AIDS (UNAIDS)
20 Avenue Appia CH-1211 Geneva 27 Switzerland
Web site: www.unaids.org

UNAIDS is a joint venture of various organizations, including UNICEF, the World Health Organization, the World Bank, and many others. Through UNAIDS they help mount and support an expanded response to AIDS—one that engages the efforts of many sectors and partners from government and civil society. They publish numerous reports about global efforts to eradicate AIDS and treat people living with HIV.

Mothers' Voices
150 W. Flagler St., Ste. 2825 Miami, FL 33130
(305) 347-5467 • Web site: www.mothersvoices.org

Mothers' Voices is composed of mothers concerned about AIDS. It works for AIDS education to prevent the transmission of HIV, the promotion of safer sexual behavior, research for better treatments and a cure, and compassion for every person living with HIV and AIDS. The group publishes fact sheets, a newsletter, events information, and other information on its Web site.

National AIDS Fund

729 Fifteenth St. NW, 9th Fl. Washington, DC 20005-1511
(202) 408-4848 • Web site: www.aidsfund.org

The National AIDS Fund seeks to eliminate HIV as a major health and social problem. Its members work in partnership with the public and private sectors to provide care and to prevent new infections in communities and in the workplace by means of advocacy, grants, research, and education. Numerous reports and other publications are available through the group's Web site.

National Association of People with AIDS (NAPWA)

8401 Colesville Rd., Ste. 505 Silver Spring, MD 20910
(240) 247-0880 • Web site: www.napwa.org

The NAPWA is an organization that represents people with HIV. Its members believe that it is the inalienable right of every person with HIV to have health care, to be free from discrimination, to have the right to a dignified death, to be adequately housed, to be protected from violence, and to travel and immigrate regardless of country of origin or HIV status.

National Institute of Allergies and Infectious Diseases (NIAID)

Office of Communications 6610 Rockledge Dr., MSC 6612
Bethesda, MD 20892-6612 • (866) 284-4107
Web site: www.niaid.nih.gov

The NIAID is a component of the National Institutes of Health. It supports research aimed at preventing, diagnosing, and treating diseases such as AIDS and tuberculosis as well as allergic conditions like asthma. NIAID publishes educational materials, booklets, and fact sheets that cover AIDS drug and vaccine development and the effect of AIDS on women, children, and minority populations.

Sex Information and Education Council of the United States (SIECUS)

90 John St., Ste. 704 New York, NY 10038
(212) 819-9770 • Web site: www.siecus.org

SIECUS is an organization of educators, physicians, social workers, and others who support the individual's right to acquire knowledge of sexuality and who encourage responsible sexual behavior. The council promotes comprehensive sex education for all children that includes AIDS education, teaching about homosexuality, and instruction about contraceptives and sexually transmitted diseases.

Bibliography

Books

Barnett, Tony, and Alan Whiteside, *AIDS in the Twenty-first Century: Disease and Globalization: 2nd ed.* New York: Palgrave Macmillan, 2006.

Behrman, Greg, *The Invisible People: How the U.S. Has Slept Through the Global AIDS Pandemic.* New York: Free Press, 2009.

Brown, Marvelyn, and Courtney Martin, *The Naked Truth: Young, Beautiful, and (HIV) Positive.* London: Harper Paperbacks, 2008.

Engel, Jonathan, *The Epidemic: A Global History of AIDS.* Washington, DC: Smithsonian, 2006.

Epstein, Helen, *The Invisible Cure: Why We Are Losing the Fight Against AIDS in Africa.* New York: Picador, 2008.

Gallant, Joel, *100 Questions and Answers About HIV and AIDS.* Sudbury, MA: Jones and Bartlett, 2007.

Hunter, Susan, *AIDS in America.* New York: Palgrave Macmillan, 2009.

Nolen, Stephanie, *28: Stories of AIDS in Africa.* New York: Walker, 2008.

Pisani, Elizabeth, *The Wisdom of Whores: Bureaucrats, Brothels and the Business of AIDS.* New York: Norton, 2009.

Shilts, Randy, *And the Band Played On: Politics, People, and the AIDS Epidemic.* Rev. ed. New York: St. Martin's Griffin, 2007.

Periodicals

CNN.com, "Interview with Anthony Fauci, Despite 'AIDS Fatigue,' Americans Should Care," November 30, 2007. http://edition.cnn.com/2007/HEALTH/conditions/11/30/aids.day.fauci/index.html.

Economist, "Sex and Sensibility," March 19, 2009. www
.economist.com/opinion/displaystory.cfm?story_
id = 13326176.

Erbe, Bonnie, "Pope's Dangerous AIDS Message in Africa:
No Condoms," *U.S. News & World Report*, March 18,
2009. www.usnews.com/blogs/erbe/2009/03/18/
popes-dangerous-aids-message-in-africa-no-
condoms.html.

Fletcher, Michael A., "Bush Has Quietly Tripled Aid to
Africa: Increase in Funding to Impoverished Continent
Is Viewed as Altruistic or Pragmatic," *Washington Post*,
December 31, 2006.

Holtgrave, David, "To End America's AIDS Crisis, Reinvest
in Prevention," *Huffington Post*, May 11, 2009. www
.huffingtonpost.com/david-holtgrave/to-end-
americas-aids-cris_b_201838.html.

Ishaug, Mark, "High Hopes Await Obama in HIV/AIDS
Fight," *Huffington Post*, December 1, 2008. www
.huffingtonpost.com/mark-ishaug/high-hopes-await-
obama-in_b_147226.html.

Kamau, Pius, "Pope's Words Poison: Comments on AIDS
and Condoms Unfortunate," *Denver Post*, March 21,
2009.

Lane, T., "In South Africa, Wives' HIV Prevention Beliefs
Affect Condom Use with Spouse," *International Family
Planning Perspectives*, September 2004.

London Times, "Pope's Attack on Condoms Sickens AIDS
Campaigners," March 18, 2009.

Martin, Roland S., "Pope Wrong on Condoms," CNN.
com, March 18, 2009. www.cnn.com/2009/POL
ITICS/03/18/martin.condoms/index.html.

Myers, Kevin, "Why Pope's Right That Condoms Won't
Solve African AIDS Crisis," *Telegraph* (Belfast), March
27, 2009. www.belfasttelegraph.co.uk/opinion/why-
popersquos-right-that-condoms-wonrsquot-solve-
african-aids-crisis-14246666.html.

Nixon, Ron, "Bottom Line for (Red)," *New York Times*,
February 6, 2008. www.nytimes.com/2008/02/06/

business/06red.html?_r = 2&scp = 1&sq = bottom + lin
e&st = nyt&oref = slogin.

Seattle Times, "Pope Benedict's Alternate Universe," March 19, 2009.

Toronto Star, "Papal Blind Spot on HIV," March 19, 2009.

UNAIDS, *Report on the Global AIDS Epidemic,* 2008. www.unaids.org/en/KnowledgeCentre/HIVData/ GlobalReport/2008.

Valdiserri, Ronald O., "AIDS at 25: Perspectives and Retrospectives," *Windy City Times,* June 21, 2006. www.windycitymediagroup.com/gay/lesbian/news/ ARTICLE.php?AID = 11776.

Williams, Brian, "Bono, Bobby Shriver Hope Americans See Red: Latest Effort to Help AIDS Victims in Africa Leverages Our Buying Power," MSNBC.com, October 13, 2006. www.msnbc.msn.com/id/15253887.

Web Sites

AIDS Newspaper Archive (www.aidsarchive.com). A very useful site that has the largest newspaper database of free AIDS articles online. Students can view articles chronologically or search via keyword.

The Body: Complete AIDS/HIV Resource (www.the body.com). This site contains a wealth of information for people studying HIV/AIDS and for those living with the disease. Links to breaking news, speeches, medical releases, and other information are readily available. The site also features blogs written by people living with HIV/AIDS and an Ask the Expert section in which doctors and other specialists answer questions about the disease.

Centers for Disease Control and Prevention HIV/ AIDS Page (www.cdc.gov/hiv). This authoritative site provides a wealth of information on various at-risk groups in America. Students will find statistical information, fact sheets, newsletters, and other useful information.

Health, Education, AIDS Liaison (HEAL) (www.heal toronto.com). This site is sponsored by a nonprofit organization of volunteers who question many common beliefs surrounding HIV and AIDS. For example, they question the idea that antiviral drugs, designed to eradicate HIV, are as safe or effective as has been widely claimed. Their site contains more information on issues related to commonly held assumptions regarding HIV/AIDS.

(Red) Campaign Web Site (www.joinred.com/Splash .aspx). Information about product sponsors, celebrity endorsements, and ways money raised from (Red) product purchases is used.

Index

Picture Credits

AP Images, 16, 19, 25, 29, 34, 36, 45, 48, 51

Image copyright Kuzma, 2010. Used under license from
  Shutterstock.com, 14

Luke MacGregor/Reuters/Landov, 40

Steve Zmina, 22, 26, 30, 35, 43, 50, 52

About the Editor

Lauri S. Friedman earned her bachelor's degree in religion and political science from Vassar College in Poughkeepsie, New York. Her studies there focused on political Islam. Friedman has worked as a nonfiction writer, a newspaper journalist, and an editor for more than ten years. She has extensive experience in both academic and professional settings.

Friedman is the founder of LSF Editorial, a writing and editing business in San Diego. She has edited and authored numerous publications for Greenhaven Press on controversial social issues such as Islam, genetically modified food, women's rights, school shootings, gay marriage, and Iraq. Every book in the *Writing the Critical Essay* series has been under her direction or editorship, and she has personally written more than twenty titles in the series. She was instrumental in the creation of the series, and played a critical role in its conception and development.